"Part punk zine, part battle cry, this debut wields teen angst and riot grrrl rage like a spiked dog collar or a fist."
—*KIRKUS REVIEWS*

"A deeply personal mythology interwoven with the fibers of LA, simultaneously shaped by and shaping our city, Nikki Darling's *Fade Into You* is a poetic portrait of a young girl's life in the Angeleno multiverse."
—ALICE BAG, author of *Violence Girl*

"A coming-of-age story set in the dreamy wasteland of nineties Los Angeles, *Fade Into You* hypnotizes with its poetry and slang, the edgy mystery of girl friendships and skater crushes, overworked and unavailable parents, the uselessness of education and crucial importance of gossip. Nikki Darling shows us the real world, wrapped in a stoner haze, through the eyes of a girl on the cusp of sinking or swimming. Beautiful."
—MICHELLE TEA, author of *Against Memoir: Complaints, Confessions & Criticisms*

"Nikki Darling captures the layers of being and not being in one of the great world cities, Los Angeles, but moreover of the San Gabriel Valley. Darling understands the sterile streets tinged with deadly angst, the disarming city that hits you between the eyes, the way voices and beats stream out of yawning windows and rolled-down car windows. She sings and shouts from an LA no Hollywood can touch."
—LUIS J
Always Running: La Vida

"A glorious illumination of the dark corners of teen trouble, *Fade Into You* tangles Chicano cultural inheritance, nascent punk self-discovery, and kid truth in a stoned haze. Darling's vivid prose is transporting."

—JESSICA HOPPER, author of *The First Collection of Criticism by a Living Female Rock Critic*

"Nikki Darling and I are in love with the same girl, California, and Nikki has written a love letter to her in the form of a hella vernacular novel of which I'm envious AF. Reading *Fade Into You* is like tasting an orange grown in this magical place: you can savor the SoCal sun on every page, and this sun tastes tangier, dirtier, and more glamorous than it does anywhere else on this weird, stupid earth. Taste it and get that Vitamin C."

—MYRIAM GURBA, author of *Mean*

fade into you

fade into you

NIKKI DARLING

FEMINIST
PRESS
AT THE CITY UNIVERSITY
OF NEW YORK
NEW YORK CITY

Published in 2018 by the Feminist Press
at the City University of New York
The Graduate Center
365 Fifth Avenue, Suite 5406
New York, NY 10016

feministpress.org

First Feminist Press edition 2018

This book was made possible thanks to a grant from the New York State
Council on the Arts with the support of Governor Andrew M. Cuomo and the
New York State Legislature.

First printing November 2018

Edited by Michelle Tea

Cover and text design by Suki Boynton

Library of Congress Cataloging-in-Publication Data
Names: Darling, Nikki, 1980- author.
Title: Fade into you / Nikki Darling.
Description: First Feminist Press edition. | New York, NY : Feminist Press,
   2018.
Identifiers: LCCN 2018028245 (print) | LCCN 2018029183 (ebook) | ISBN
   9781936932429 (e-book) | ISBN 9781936932412 (trade pbk.)
Classification: LCC PS3604.A7464 (ebook) | LCC PS3604.A7464 F33 2018
(print)
   | DDC 813/.6--dc23
LC record available at https://lccn.loc.gov/2018028245

*For all the girls that feel like women
and all the women that feel like girls
and everyone in between.*

fade into you

It was only there at the interface
that we could see each other.
See? We wanted to touch.
I wished I could become
pulsing color, pure sound, bodiless as she.

—GLORIA ANZALDÚA

Strange little girl, where are you going?

—THE STRANGLERS

hop the fence into an empty lot and walk toward the main road. Think it's Garvey, can't be sure. Kick some smashed-up Olde E 40s across the ripped-up asphalt. Cancer butts and orange juice caps, old doll hair and other debris that's floated down from the city clog up the cracks. The pink stucco apartments and motels stuffed into the flat expanse like miniature huts. Blinking *vacant, vacant*. The rainbow flags around the car dealerships flap underneath bright neon lights. "Three Days" by Jane's Addiction is playing on my Walkman and I feel like I'm in a movie, like I'm an assassin. I skip through the dark street and wait in the middle of the road as souped-up rockets and old beaters honk and swerve around me. Raise my arms, cigarette hanging from my lips like some outlaw. I'm smiling. It's clenched there all tobaccoey between my teeth. I've got someplace to be or maybe nowhere to go. My head is a hive of vibration and sonic awesomeness. The drums are like *tat a tat tat, tat a tat tat*, and then Dave Navarro squeals all over it with a sharp splice of noise. Perry Farrell slithers in behind. *All now with wings!* Fly around me, motherfuckers! Fly around me like I'm not even here! Like I'm not even a person in this world at all.

×

Mom is in the kitchen grabbing her keys and throwing an apple into her purse. She's tired and doesn't look at me. I look up from my bowl of cereal. I'm wearing the clothes I wore yesterday and I know she's trying to figure out if I just put them on again or never took them off. She was up when I came home last night. She didn't come into the living room when the door opened like she sometimes does. I'm never really in trouble for anything. It's more of a negotiation. Come on, she'd say. Just throw me a bone. But I'm not a bone thrower. Not anymore.

"Gotta go," she says hovering near the door. "Go to school."

"Duh."

"Not duh. Go."

"Yeah. Okay."

She shakes her head softly and heads outside to the car. I stand and walk into my bedroom. It's seven thirty. A now or never sort of hour.

×

"What's going on?" I ask, shoving my way toward the front of the gathering crowd at the entrance to King Hall, the main building at Cal State LA where our school is housed.

We go to the LA County High School for the Arts. Like
Fame but here in LA and no one dances in the caf to "Hot
Lunch" or stops traffic to boogie down on yellow taxicab
roofs, mainly though cos we have a food court and it's LA,
you know? We all have cars. Crappy ones, we're teenagers,
but we drive. I can see the tops of our 1970s orange-and-
yellow lockers, eighties Pirate Radio and Mark & Brian
stickers stuck to the front, KROQ through the ages, a ubiq-
uitous rainbow across genre and sex. Everybody and their
older sister loves KROQ. Power 106 stickers sprinkled
sparsely throughout, a bolder radio choice made most
often by the cool black girl dancers and straight white art
boys. Pirouetting across the mirror at lunch and bumping Aaliyah on the bus back home, pink leg warmers over
gold Adidas, sending 80087355 911 on a sticker-covered
pager. Silhouetting breasts in charcoal at break, smoking
bowls, air punching Tupac, playing Sega after school in
their game basement in North Hollywood, junior high
posters of Jim Morrison, a giant psychedelic pot leaf, and
Bob Marley behind them. Their public school teacher
mother upstairs, making them sandwiches. Dance girl,
paint boy. They ignore me anyway. I'm in musical theater.
We're sort of like the blissed-out cheerleaders on campus.
Dancing, leaping, talking loudly about Disneyland and
Barbra Streisand and how many times we saw *Phantom* at
the Dorothy Chandler when it came to town in '91, fourth
grade. The chandelier! Each year in April, during the week
Disneyland parade scouts come for summer cast-member
auditions, we take over campus with our costumes and

over-the-top talking hands. We make warm-up noises and click our tongues in the locker hallway. We transition from being marginally annoying to across-campus hated. I'm not really like that, though. Not anymore. I'm more of a Bob Fosse *Cabaret, Jesus Christ Superstar* type of brooding musical theater gal these days, but I mean that in the depressed, burned-out way. If someone in musical theater could be, you know, depressed and burned out. That's me. I'm sixteen. *Sing to me my angel of music!*

Anyway, right now there's shouting, and the crowd grows as my classmates run toward us from King Hall. Kids running late have bottlenecked the giant vertical stairs. Everyone starts backing down so the paramedics can pass. I had asked what was going on sort of rhetorically, but now I'm looking for someone to legitimately tell me what's up because this entire scene is very three-dimensional.

Mike grabs my arm and pulls me toward him. "Get over here, look," he says pointing at a stretcher being carried down the stairs by two medics. I crane my neck and look down the many flights of stairs to where an ambulance flashes red. "It's Claire Chang, she was cutting at her arm during class and Lisa told Mr. York and he called 911."

"Was she trying to kill herself?" I ask, knowing that she wasn't and following the crowd now winding down the steps.

"No, I don't think so." The medics stop walking and then so do we. All present thump to a halt. Claire sits up on the gurney and we watch, like even though she plays clarinet and is in the music department, this is the greatest monologue of her life and we've been invited to her private theater. VIP. She turns her head slowly, Regan from *The Exorcist*, eyes focused and calm. Last year she was expelled for bringing a nitrous tank to the Monterey Jazz Festival and getting the ensemble high minutes before their performance. This past summer, angry with an ex-boyfriend, she drove her Miata to his family's house while they were on vacation, stuck a hose in the front door mail slot, and turned on the water full blast. Her sophomore year she was arrested and taken to juvenile hall for beating a boy over the head with a skateboard after he got her naked in a bedroom at a party then burned her clothes inside a paper bag. She's always been cool to me. In fact, she's one of the best girls I know. I look at her arm and the thin safety-pin scratches almost make me guffaw. She was bored, mindlessly dragging a lazy safety pin across her arm, chewing her pencil. Claire has just transformed into a witch, a warning to others who might embrace her path to freedom. I look up dutifully, in awe, in wonder.

"Each and every one of you," she begins, her blue-black hair crowned and hovering about her head, flames licking up toward the calm blue sky, "will remember me for the rest of your lives."

×

In History later Principal Gaines walks in and we look up and across the room in unison. The entire day has been

7

a little jumpy, shifty. "Mr. Sorenson," he says, nodding, "I need to pull you away from class."

"Is everything all right?" he asks, shutting his book and walking toward the door.

"Yes, everything's fine, I need to ask you some questions about," he clears his throat and leans in, "*Claire Chang.*" He whispers this but of course we can all hear him because he doesn't actually care to be mindful of her privacy.

"Of course."

Mr. Gaines opens the door for Mr. Sorenson to follow and he does. In the hallway are two officers, hands on their belts. The door swings shut and . . .

×

"Did you hear what happened to Claire?" asks Chelo, pulling a bobby pin from between her teeth and parting my hair with one hand, looking for a place to shove it in my head as if trying to pick a point at random on a map.

"No," I answer, sitting up.

"Hold still," she says, stoned, still looking.

"Just pin the bangs," I say.

"Oh, yeah." She jams the pin in at my temple, certainly drawing blood.

"Jesus, Chelo," I say, rubbing my cranium. "Cool it, vampire."

"They took her away. Locked her up for good."

"Shut up. They locked her up two years ago and she still didn't get kicked out. She wins awards and shit."

"Don't matter, and hell, they did more than kick home-girl out, she's locked up in Pasadena at that girls' center."

"What girls' center?" I ask, rolling my eyes and giving heavy *ugh*.

"Dude, you are not listening to me. She went crazy. They put her in the crazy house. The cathouse of death, yo. She's like, you know, Frances Farmer now, or whatever."

"You are so wigged out."

"Fine, don't believe me, but watch it, the city's investigating and they're looking closely at everyone's records, absences, shit like that."

"You don't know that."

"Like hell I don't. Renee works in the office. She heard them talking about it, Ms. Martínez and Mr. Gaines, in his office, this afternoon. They're really tripped out about this thing. It doesn't look good for the school. Their blue ribbons and shit."

"Because Claire cut herself with a safety pin the police are investigating everyone?"

"Dude, you saw them pull Sorenson out of class. Plus, it was more than that. She carved a word—no, a *phrase*," she says pointedly, smiling.

"Okay, what?"

"Fuck. The. World."

"No way. I saw her arm."

"Did you? I mean, fuck the world? That's pretty badass. She's badass. I'll give her that."

I might have seen it, I might not have. I'm not sure anymore. "So then what?"

"She's been committed, probably cos she's got priors. I think they're gonna start kicking kids out or doing evaluations with doctors and shit. I mean, after that girl from choir tried to bleed herself in the prop room, and now Claire—"

"Stop," I say, looking down at my hands.

"Come to class, that's all I'm saying. Don't get wiggy in the hallway."

I swallow hard and smile. I'm always wondering, is now the time to tell Chelo, or like my family do I just carry on like nothing happened?

I'm sitting on a tall white plastic laundry basket in Chelo's closet, queenlike on a pile of dirty jeans and socks, blowing bud smoke out the window, swishing it around with my hand. The closet is hot and smoky like a high school gym locker, like in *Carrie* before she gets pelted with tampons. Before the pilot light goes on inside her brain. *Your mom's a witch, bitch!*

Chelo flips her fire-engine Manic Panic hair and leans in close, holding the small silver scissor sideways near my forehead, like a professional. "Bettie Page was a puta," she says, changing the subject, and I love her.

"But she had good hair."

"And she gave good head."

"And found Jesus in the end."

"Your roots are showing."

"We're writing a poem."

She snips and small black pieces flutter into the basket, on top of a vintage Disneyland sweatshirt. The kind

Lydia Lunch wore in the seventies. The kind we spend all day on Melrose looking for in old barrels of mildewed army jackets at the Melrose Punk Store, a.k.a. the Salvation Army. Near the Hassidic retirement home. Near the chained-up dog, near the skateboarder who sniffed glue from that lunch bag. Near the ghost of rock 'n' roll. By the guts of some dumb bird. Some dumb pigeon. Who knows what.

"Your roots are bleached and black."

"I need to buy more dye. I think I did 'em good. Look." She holds out a small oval hand mirror. My face, my strange, crooked face. Even with all this other muck I still look like me. That's all that counts I guess.

"It doesn't even look like you. You look hot."

Black bob, short black bangs, Cleopatra eyeliner, penciled eyebrows, and outlined brown lips. Fire-engine apple virginity-ripped red. All lacquered and stained.

"I look like a chola."

"You *are* a chola, puta. A psychobilly chola."

"A white girl in disguise. And what are you?"

"Half-white, puta. Don't forget your familia." She throws hands and I push them away with a roll of the eyes. "I'm punk rock," she says.

"Punk rockers don't wear Gunne Sax, daisies in their hair, and combat boots."

"Fine. I'm me." She brings her hands to her chin and opens them like fans, like wings, as if she's presenting herself to me, a human offering. A teenage girl head.

"Then I'm me, too."

"If you say so, Mousie," she says, referencing *Mi Vida Loca*, and winks at me.

"Shut up, stupid," I say and we laugh.

×

My grandpa's from Echo Park. He grew up on Carroll Avenue in a run-down apartment. They'd come over from Canada, the part that's above Washington. They were English, Spanish. The last name changed somewhere along the way. Became Darling. Can't tell you how exactly, but I've made up tons of stories. Spread them thick around town. It's a thing to do when people ask and they always do. Truthfully? I think the Darlings were just ancient English boot makers or something. Which would make sense since my great-great-grandfather started the first denim factory in downtown at the turn of the century. But the Canada stuff doesn't matter anyway because my grandpa's family never talked about before California. They'd cut that part out like a cancer. We burned the tip like a shoelace, made a hard, gnarled new closure so the past wouldn't unravel.

Here's the skinny and you've got no choice to believe me, but I'll tell you what, I wouldn't lie about it anyway because I think it's cool. We're in the first California social registry. With the Californios. When Junípero Serra and his long lineage of padres took off down the highway of old news and Pío Pico rode into town with his books and architecture, my great-great-great-grandfather stood in line to record our shit. We exist. I'll tell you that.

Since then it's been endless birthing of blond-haired, blue-eyed, devil-could-care Darling surfer boys riding their bikes down to the shore, along the LA river, telling girls that being a Darling was no big deal. Slipping bikini straps off golden shoulders, pressing the ladies into the leathered upholstery of unlocked VW backseats. Riding crooked on the way back home, the orange sun on their peeling backs, laughing about what poor dope had to wipe their scuzz off the inside of his windows.

Alta California, my girl. My woman. Queen. Open your legs and give birth to this dirty nonsense. This muck-rucking nest of black magic and flickering film reels. You unforgiving greedy plot of flowers. You empty desert. You cotton ball dipped in sand. My history lies with you. I'll make hands to that. I'll spray-paint my name across a slip of a boy to claim you. A stocky rod. A silver, shining, sad-eyed boy. Brown. White tube socks in Nike chanclas. Tiny pinpricks up and down his mocha arms. Yellow crust around the outside of his mouth. Thick tongue trying to moisten up. *SGV* scarred and scabbed blue into the skin. Olde English. Let's take him. Let's eat him alive, you and me.

×

Lydia pages from the Target in Alhambra. She wants us to pick her up, and Chelo's down.

"I don't know, man," I say, lying back on her bed. The sheet with the constellation pattern on it that she uses as a curtain is pulled up and hooked on a nail. Bright afternoon

13

sunlight cuts across our bodies like the slow lid of a coffin moving in to entomb us. "I can't miss Arts."

"We won't miss Arts, okay? It's like," she holds up the pager, "two thirty."

"By the time we go all the way to Alhambra and drive all the way back to school it'll be past four. I can't miss anyway. I have a monologue due."

"Well fuck," she says, lying on her stomach and kicking her legs up, pulling the crust off a piece of cinnamon toast we'd made in the kitchen. "What about Lydia?"

"What about her? No one told her dumb ass to go suck cock in Vincent Lugo Park."

"I could eat this shit all day."

"I can't miss. If I miss I'm on probation."

"All right," she says, swinging her legs to the edge of the bed and sitting up. "Lemme brush my teeth and we'll go back."

"Well, don't you have class too?"

She shrugs her shoulders. "Just Figure Drawing. Nothing serious or nothing. Besides, you're the dummy that misses academics all the time. If you paced yourself you could chill more, but each time you gotta sneeze, you skip out. This is your own fault."

"What the hell is this right now? It doesn't look like you're in class either."

"Yeah, but my ass isn't on probation."

"Exactly, come on!"

She gets up and disappears down the hallway toward the bathroom. I roll on my stomach and stare at the Drew Barrymore postcard taped to the wall. Drew's hair is short and bleached and daisies are pinned in it. She's licking her bottom lip and holding her titties. The butterfly tattoo above her happy trail looks soft and fleshy.

"Yummy," Chelo says, licking her fingers and holding a new piece of cinnamon toast.

"Dude, you are majorly malfunctioned."

"What?" she says, getting hard with me. "Fuck you. I'm faded. Don't get like that, I'll pow pow you." And she means it.

"Just hurry up, dude."

"*Hurry up, dude,*" she says mimicking my voice. In her mouth I sound like a cartoon mouse on helium. "Like whatever, majorly mal, mal estúpida. I'll drop you off in Sherman Oaks, dude, you can take the bus home."

"Probation, Chelo. Come on."

"Then you should have stayed at school, dummy."

"Please."

"Fine! I said I would. Chill, crazy. I'm eating, okay? It's not even three yet."

I sigh and sit up, stuff CDs I brought over into my backpack.

"Ugh," she says, exhaling. "You're such an elevator operator. Come on." She grabs her Star Wars lunch box and heads for the front door.

"Thank you, thank you."

"Whatever. You have to tell Lydi why we ditched her ass, though."

"Whatever. Fine."

"You're a burn, man."

I'm going through Chelo's tapes in the glove compartment looking for something decent to listen to.

"Put on the Lilliput," she says, reaching over my lap and fishing through the pile. I look down and the bottom pocket of her hoodie moves.

"What the fuck is that?" I shout, jumping back. She grabs the Lilliput and shoves it in the cassette player.

"It's Pinwheel Loco. Chill."

"You brought the fucking hamster?"

"Whatever. I'm dropping your whiny bitch ass off and getting Lydi."

"So you brought your hamster?"

"What is wrong with you today, man? Is it your moon times? Are you PMSing? Why do you *even* care?"

"Well, can't he die?"

"What?" she asks, getting all twisted up in the face. "No. Why the fuck would he die? Do I look like Lennie from *Mice and Estúpidos*?"

"Well, what are you going to do with him?"

"Put him in my backpack. He can breathe, it's got holes in it."

I shake my head.

"Just get out when it's time to get out. I'll call you never."

"Whatever, dude," I say, leaning my head against the glass.

"Swear to god you're a bitch."

"Whatever, dude." I look down at my nails and start to bite.

"Don't spit that shit in here."

I scrunch up my face and look at her. *What?* I ask without words. "You've got fucking Taco Bell wrappers on the floor."

"Yeah, but those are nails. Swallow that shit or roll down the window."

"I can't believe you even eat that crap."

"I like the cinnamon twists, *bitch*," she hisses.

"That's a taco wrapper, grosso."

"Man, why you gotta be such a bummer bitch about everything, your way or the highway, right? Next time don't even ditch with me. I'm tired of chauffeuring your ass all over LA. Enjoy your two-hour bus ride home."

We pull into F lot. Chelo grabs the hand brake and the whole thing dies in a lurch. I pull the seat back and grab my stuff. We flip each other off and I slam the door. Head for the long stairway toward campus and look back, watch her white '68 Super Beetle zoom and sputter toward Valley Boulevard. Whatever, man. Whatever by so much. Hope your fucking hamster dies.

×

I drag my tired ass up the driveway toward the mailbox. Mom's tulips are blooming white, buttercup yellow, and it's clear and bright outside. I was so upset after my fight with Chelo I skipped Arts anyway and got on the B43 toward home. Large wayward clouds move slow over our street, detouring before they turn into pirate ships, head out toward Never Never Land. I always check for *Movieline* magazine or *The New Yorker*. We actually get six different magazines in the mail, plus the newspaper, but those are the only two I like. I'm obsessed with *Movieline* critic Stephen Rebello. On Sunday mornings—not so much anymore and I kinda wish we still did this, so I guess when I was younger—Sunday mornings, Mom, Parsley, and I would sit in the big oak mission chairs, the *LA Times* spread at our feet, like we were secret agents trying to figure out some master plan, one of us leaning over the fanned pages searching for the Style section, or the Calendar section, or the *Sunday Magazine* insert with the glossy touch. I still read the funnies up until our tradition stopped. Mom would make peppermint tea, a plate of scrambled eggs, chopped-up bacon, green onions, a dollop of sour cream, and some RO*TEL, and we'd scoop it up with tortillas. The entire day, sunrise to sunset in our pj's, reading in silence with one another, together, nary a word spoken yet the afternoon consumed by words.

There are no magazines, but there is a letter from school addressed to Mom and I can tell it's one of those disciplinary ones, most likely reporting that I've been put on probation for ditching. I contemplate hiding it, placing it in my backpack, she'll never be the wiser, but decide to leave it, as a dare. See if she'll do anything, say anything. Most likely she'll blow a front but nothing will actually change. Maybe she's a parenting genius and I'll grow up to be some rich lawyer, the joke on me. I stick my key in the old Craftsman lock and shove the door open with my hip.

Parsley is asleep, blinks, stretches, jumps to his feet, and walks in circles around my ankles. "Hey, buddy," I whisper, leaning down and giving his head a scratch. He follows me into the yellow kitchen, his orange head and half-bitten ear like some hobo alley gato in a comic strip, bobbing along beside me.

"You hungry?" He lets out a generous meow as if he's been waiting all day for someone to ask. "Yeah, me too." I pull some Thai leftovers out of the fridge but they look gross and old so I put them back and close the door. Walk to the cabinet and grab Parsley's dry food, put a scoop in his bowl. He's good and busy now. I walk back into the living room, pull a five out of my pocket and flop into one of the wooden mission chairs. The sun has that yellowy glow before it goes haywire rainbow before it goes navy before it goes black.

I think about grabbing garlic knots at Pietro's on the corner but don't want to walk home in the dark so I put the bill back in my pocket and sit up, go into my room, open my small wooden heart jewelry box, and unwrap a roach from a napkin. I take the wallet photos of my Ramona Convent friends out and look at them, lean against the dresser. Yuniva's quince, Luce, Marisela, and I at the Montebello Fashion Center, lips brown, eyes hard, hair bouffant. Well, except for me. I'm wearing a peach fake-cashmere Fashion 21 sweater, fifties red lips and smiling. Like some out-of-place turd, some Sherilyn Fenn greasy-faced nightmare. My braces all *der*. I look like a waitress at Johnny Rockets on Halloween. I fuck up the photo. It's been two years since I saw any of them and their faces already seem like faces from a yearbook in a thrift store, old and dated. I'm not sure if this is because I've changed so much since then or if it's because seemingly nothing ever changes and teenage girls continue on some existential loop, forever repeating the mistakes of their foremothers, their faces, eyes betraying the inner sadness of being a female human in the world. Bumped forever against a tide of information and indoctrination, the weightlessness of childhood, the supposed weightlessness of childhood, ripped like wings from the back of some disgusting bug.

Noel Campos was the one friend who wrote me a letter after I left. I mean, I could have done it too, written first, but when something hurts I want to push it as quickly into the past as possible. It leaves a heavy lump of guilt dolloped on every old acquaintance, my inadequacy at staying in touch. In my experience, distance is a thing stretching two people further apart until they can no longer see one another properly. The supposed touchstone of teenage girlhood: the moody-broody letter. The one I always write but never send.

Hey, COOCH, Noel's letter started,

Where has your stoopid ass been all year? Yeah, yeah, I know you got into that fancy art school. Hey thanks for inviting me to all those cool Hollywood parties you said you were going to invite me to. Naw, I'm just playing. But I do miss you stupid. Even if your jokes are dumb and you talk too much. You aren't funny by the way don't start letting people tell you that you are. Don't go thinking you're Roseanne Barr—Arnold?—who the hell knows, putas! All of them!

How's the Bikini Kill in those parts? It's still skimpy here, as you can imagine. Antonietta is pregnant, big surprise. She's taking next semester off. Some skunk head from Bosco. I told her, just because your ass wears a Cure shirt don't not make you a puta. She spit at me. Trashy! What a beautiful way to exhibit your point, I told her. Fuck this place. Fuck Sister P, she's been on a tear, she even brought a ruler to class and tapped desks, I was like, bitch, hit my knuckles, I'll write a letter to Gil Garcetti and have this place shut down. No, but I said it in my head. Did you find the bloody glove?! Was it up Kato Kaelin's ass? Was it up mine? Yours?

We AIDS walking this year? I'm thinking of joining ROTC, for real. Can we talk about it soon? I might be scared.

Noel–stinky SNATCH–

I exhale a thin plume of perfect smoke and dig the tiny bits of burned-out roach into the backyard dirt, my fingertips sizzling, my mind now, too, a fuzzy cloud, the sun setting into that hazy rainbow, the San Gabriel Mountains starting their slow, black outline against a blanket of sky. Not hungry anymore, just stoned. I walk to the back porch and through Mom's studio. Oasis, flower stems, raffia, Styrofoam, ceramic bowls, and her notebooks filled with intricate ikebana designs. The thing she gets paid a small bundle for. The thing she's known for, out in Bev Hills, over on the Westside, people you watch on TV ask her to do their parties and she does. No matter what time, what holiday, or what school pageant, graduation, or special event it might conflict with, she will be there, tying lilies into the braided hair of their blond children, at important dinners, dressing their Christmas trees for a holiday party, designing and redesigning centerpieces for their grand pianos that overlook canyon verandas.

When I was a child and there was no one to watch me she'd bring me to work. To these large, flat, midcentury modern, light-blue-and-white stucco masterpieces high above the city, bamboo walls and built-in bookshelves, brass door handles, and glass-framed floor-to-ceiling artworks, overlooking a bright, green-tiled pool. One time, a woman who lived in one of these multilevel architectural marvels, a spindly old thing with a puff of white, coiffed hair, a smear of orange lipstick, orange-lacquered short brittle nails, ironed gold slacks, and a cream-colored housecoat, handed me a peanut butter and jelly sandwich. "You don't have to do that," said my mother, turning to the woman from where she stood on a ladder, hanging a Christmas garland around the room.

"Oh, it's okay," smiled the woman, patting my head. Later that day, as I went searching for a bathroom, the sandwich crusts still balled in my fist, peanut butter and jelly on my fingertips and wrists, I tripped on my shoelace, caught myself on the wall and a large painting of a swimming pool, very much like the one outside, a small splash of water painted in its center, a green palm tree top swaying in a brush-struck aqua breeze. The woman hurried into the room, horrified, and yelled, "That's a

Hockney!" then grabbed my elbow, yanking me to my feet, got low in my face, and spit a warning to either sit down and remain seated and not touch another thing or wait in my mother's car. "This is the sort of thanks we get nowadays for generosity!" she huffed. "Watch your child!" she warned my mother, and went back outside, pulling giant gold praying mantis sunglasses over her face. She picked up a small crystal glass filled low with ice cubes and dark liquor, and sat, taking small sips, looking into the dry hills, while inside I cried quietly and in a hiss Mom promised to smack me if I did not sit down.

I walk back through my house, stoned. Parsley asleep again, I open the front door and head back to the mailbox, take the letter from school, and stand it perpendicular in the box, so there is no way that she can miss it. I take the other mail, bills, and walk them back inside, put them in the key bowl where I always put the mail, so she knows I've brought it in. I've got the itch to leave again, drive around the shrubby Altadena hills, perhaps park at Zorthian Ranch and smoke a joint. This way she at least knows I've been home.

I meander aimlessly toward the back of the house, into her bedroom, and to the closet where she keeps the old seventies sewing box filled with family photos. Drag my finger along the scalloped wall, the wooden Quaker vanity, the Hopi masks that frame the bathroom doorway. When I am bored and wistful or whatever else, I spend my time on the floor searching through the pictures, getting lost in the past, before I arrived, wondering who the people are and were, people I say I love and who claim to love me in return.

I feel my sister around me. She's in my hands, holding an eighth-grade graduation plaque, beaming, eyes bright and full of accomplishment, my parents in an early eighties corduroy jacket and a silk suit dress, my mother's artistic inclinations coming out in her bold pairing of a bright turquoise bolo tie carved into a dragon and red silk tie-dyed scarf around the purple waist of her suit. Lyla with my parents, mining for fool's gold in the American River, not far from the commune they came and went from, all in seventies denim bell-bottoms and baseball-cut tees. Lyla holding a cup, drinking the blood of Christ at her first communion in New Mexico, eyes shining and turned upward toward the cross of Jesus—and then with me, a baby, a scowl on her face, sallow and shrinking into the yellow wall of our old home. And then she's gone. And then it's only me.

In the lack my sister is heavy, ever present, and breathing, trying to tell me something. I cover my ears, squeeze my eyes, and shut her out, convinced I've gone crazy, and yet, still I return hoping to learn what? Something I don't know.

×

"Hey, wait up," I call, jog down the locker hallway. Chelo stops and spins around. Her face is all *yeah, what*. She crosses her arms. "I'm real sorry about last week." She rubs her toe into the hallway tile, squints at me, and is silent.

"Why?" she asks.

"Gosh god, why what?"

"Why are you sorry?"

"Because I was a megabitch, okay? I'm sorry I made my ditching your problem and then was you know . . ."

"An elevator operator."

"Yeah, okay, an elevator operator."

"Bringing everybody down."

"Bringing everybody down. God, okay, I'm sorry."

She bursts into a big smile and starts laughing. "Hey-seuss! You should see your face. Dang you felt real bad. Nah it's cool. Brush 'em, brush 'em, brush 'em!" she says, imitating Jan from *Grease*.

"Look at me, I'm Sandra Dee!"

"That was so pale-man of you. Don't colonize my car again."

"No, man. Never. Eat what you want."

"I will. I do. Hey, let's get out of here."

"Yes, please!" She grabs my hand and we run into the sunshine and toward the F lot steps, descending in a flurry toward her car, a waiting vehicle of change.

We're at Bennie's house, Chelo's cousin. He lives in Lincoln Heights and we go over there sometimes cos he's got weed and lets us smoke and hang out, and because his friends are pretty cool and he's into rock and roll and we're into rock and roll and his friends are sexy. They're seniors and we're juniors and some of them are a little older and it's better than my house which is empty, boring, far away, and covered in antique things that can break. Or Chelo's house with her parents at work and where her sister Adelicia and Adel's baby live. Bennie has albums and reggae and an old Impala in the backyard that we sit in listening to Lords of Acid, "Marijuana in Your Brain," and get goofy. Bennie's friends are ravers, and they always have these rad fliers for gatherings with names like JuJu Beats and Nocturnal Wonderland, PEZ dispensers filled with Special K, JNCO pants, and plastic rainbow chains, pacifiers, and candy necklaces. Mixtapes with DJs named Paulina Taylor and CandyKrush spin these foot-spazzy beats. We get high and sway kind of silly. Lords of Acid demand that we *just blow*. So we do. Sucking down joint after joint, getting dizzy snorting up K, and acting out our fantasies of sixties rebellion.

Bennie is also super hot but because Chelo is more or less my best friend I can't go after him, not that it would matter anyway cos no one is ever after me. Especially Bennie, who has every punk rock Betty hanging around waiting in line. Pick of the Bettys he's got. Oh yeah, he's also an artist and has a giant notebook he tags in and draws pencil drawings of Aztec heads and rainbows in pastel. He uses those fat paint markers and sometimes Chelo and I steal a few and huff them in the park, laughing and stumbling. His work is good. He's not as good as Chelo though, who after three years at LACHSA is trained and on her way to being a real fine artist in the sense that she will one day have a gallerist and her influences are wide and developed. Oh yeah. Chelo is a terrific painter. I suppose I waited a really long time to reveal that. Chelo can paint. Like a boss.

Bennie's dad (Chelo's uncle) is a director. He made some Radical activist films in the seventies/eighties with the Chicano art collective Asco and sometimes walks in from meetings in which he and other still-kicking seventies La Raza walkout radicals are trying to autonomize El Sereno and says "wassup" and that he just brought home tacos and Topo Chico and us kids can "help ourselves." One time I went over and Cheech as in *Cheech* was there, dropping off some fliers and picking up a painting. I stood in the hallway of their living room, mouth open, high and freaking out, heart beating like *boom boom boom* until Chelo shoved me toward Bennie's room and hissed, "Be cool." The short long of it is, it's a great place to be after school when we've both actually made it to the end of the school day and want someplace to chill.

"Check it out," says Bennie, popping *The Wizard of Oz* into the VCR. "Chelly, put on *Dark Side*." He motions to his stack of records and she jumps up and grabs it.

"Arturo said that if you watch *Oz* and listen to *Dark Side* at the same time, it matches up. Sounds tight."

"Damn, this cover," she says, turning it over.

"It's the shit." The rainbow eye zooming out of the pyramid of the moon makes everything else on this earth seem small and inconsequential. It truly is the shit. Bennie pulls the record out, puts it on, drops the needle, and Roger Waters and David Gilmour float into our existence.

Dorothy and Toto wake up in black and white. We light a doob, lie on our backs, and peek over our feet at the Oz beast, puff passing as the guitars and cash machines wail and cha-ching.

In 1973 the Laserium in Van Nuys created laser technology and Griffith Observatory hired them to make a show. The way the story goes is that the observatory's attendance was low and they wanted to hip it up. It was '77 and *Dark Side of the Moon* had just been released, was psychedelic, and probably seemed like the natural choice. Only thing they didn't count on was that it would be such a hit they'd have to offer three shows a day. Matinees started almost immediately and ditching class to see the *Dark Side* lasers became a local kid tradition. Eventually, as the decades passed and the city fell into disrepair and white flight grabbed the Eastside and San Gabriel Valley by the throat, city maintenance lost money and White Fence and Hazard popped up on every corner and Rodney King was beat down in the street and smoke and fire filled South LA and the El Monte Flores kissed the earth with blood and Northridge shook loose from its roots and O. J. took the citrus city hostage and the Raiders sailed away, Rampart bubbled up from the tar pits of corruption and baby diapers weren't uncommon on the grounds of Disneyland, Magic Mountain became a battlefield of bangers and the people of El Pueblo de Nuestra Señora la Reina de los Ángeles came out of their homes to stare as the sun became eclipsed by the moon, the observatory grew empty and teenagers tagged the seats and carved their initials into the wood armrests and the soda machine dripped yellow and the Tesla coil grew faint and the ceilings cracked and we showed up to sit and laugh and throw cigarettes at one another across the empty theater, our turn to take in the mythic lasers of our older siblings' youth. You raise the blade you make the change. There's someone in my head but it's not me. And if there are cloudbursts and thunder in your ear and no one seems to hear, just tap your heels together three times and say, "There's no place like home."

×

We crash Chelo's house after Bennie's and her parents are on the porch smoking doobs.

"Hey, come over here," calls her dad as we walk up the cement path to their white stucco craftsman. My dad loves to talk about how in the eighties "the Mexicans" stuccoed the beautiful homes of his youth, even though I'd be sitting next to him, being half-Mexican. He just appreciates architecture, "It's simply stating fact, Nicole." We have always been just two people, my dad and I, sometimes sharing space.

Baby-girl toys and a plastic Playskool giraffe faded from years of sitting outdoors, its cowboy-sticker seat brittle and disintegrating, reflect a foggy light from the bright sun. Her dad stubs out his doob and her mom follows. They give a cursory half-hearted swish of already dissipated smoke. Chelo sits in her dad's lap and lays her head on his chest. His beige Dickies have been ironed at the creases and his wifebeater appears adhered to his glowing body, as if slowly being absorbed by his glossy skin. Everything has taken on a dreamy patina and I sit on the crumbling river-stone porch and look up at a pair of pigeons nested in the wooden beams of the house, bits of brown palm frond and white takeout napkins peeking out from the attic lattice. In the distance, long palm trees, trunks like thin bent straws, are brown forms against the amber-hued sky, downtown in the distance, the black outline of shadow covering the remnants of the detailed day, blurring into dusk.

"How was school?" he asks. She sits up and shrugs.

"Okay I guess." Her legs are bent like a flopped-over puppet, her head hung low. She pushes hair out of her face and smiles and he tenderly squeezes her nose.

"Fuck you," she says, "I'm not a baby," pushing his hand away. He smacks her chin quick and sharp and she slugs him close and sharp in the thigh then gets up and looks at me. "Come on. Let's go." She opens the screen door. I follow her into the dark house as the screen swings shut, slamming behind on squeaky hinges.

"Hey, let's grab a joint," she says, and I follow her into the backyard, where on a cinder block in a sea of yellow weeds sits a paper bag from Vons. Chelo leans over it and plucks a thick perfectly rolled joint. She holds it up and squints. "Looks about right."

"Goof 'tard," I say, trying to grab it from her. She pulls it away and smiles, her tongue squeezing between her two front teeth like it sometimes does.

"Come on," she says, skip-walking toward the side of the house where we've arranged two upside-down Home Depot buckets, rolled home with our feet, for our chill zone. Beyond her house is the cemented Los Angeles River, winding toward the Sixth Street Bridge and downtown. Out here it's still the SGV, though, sleepy and tagged.

A boy about our age hops the wire fence behind Chelo's house from the ravine. "Hey," he says nodding at Chelo. "Is your sister here?"

"Who are you?" she asks, sounding tough and folding the joint into her palm.

He's wearing long black Nike sweatpants and a wife-beater, his black hair buzzed short, skin reflecting the last bits of sun, casting beams off his tanned shoulders into the distance. The moment holds me in its psychedelia. "Is Adelicia here or what?" he asks again, ignoring Chelo's attitude.

"No, she's not, and who are you?"

"I'm Dez. She knows me." I look at his arms and he's got the *EMF* for the El Monte Flores across his chest, peeking from behind his beater.

"Is she in trouble?" asks Chelo, growing bold.

"Damn, you ask a lot of questions. Who are you?" he spits, finally rising to Chelo's invitation. He straightens his shoulders and brings his hands to his waist in loose, ready fists.

"She's not here. Move," she says, brushing past him toward our buckets. "But my parents are." The handsome boy looks at me and makes no face. I hold his eye for one

31

second and he looks through me and out my back, turns around, and jumps the fence, running back into the empty riverbed.

"Who was that?" I ask, sitting beside Chelo, who sits up quickly to make sure the boy is gone.

"I'm not sure, but all these bangers have been coming around lately looking for her."

"You think she's in trouble?"

"I don't know. All I know is that she hasn't been around lately."

"I'm sure it's cool," I say.

She looks at me and blinks. "Yeah, come on, let's smoke this thing already. I'm happy to be home."

×

I'm standing in line outside Mr. Ingroff's office. He's our resident Mr. Van Driessen—you know, Beavis and Butt-Head's school counselor. Behind me is one of the girls from senior orchestra who's always wearing velvet baby-doll dresses with white satin collars and Doc Marten Mary Janes. Basically, it looks like Hot Topic threw up on her at all times. Today she is holding her small metal coffin-shaped lunch box in fingerless lace gloves. Coming down the hall from Algebra is Corinne, one of the most talented, male-desired girls on campus. She's a third-year theater ensemble member and wears her red hair swirled into a bun, her red lips always perfect, her freck-led cheeks small constellations on a peach map. What I know about her is that she had to leave school twice to go to some eating disorder place. I groan on the inside, why am I in this line of weirdos.

Mr. Ingroff sticks his head out and smiles. "Ms. Darling." He motions for me to enter. I slump low in the chair and grab my hair and twirl it. He clears his throat and sits back, sizing me up in that way that adults do when trying to discern what type of teenager you might be.

"It shows in your records that you're falling behind in your academics and arts, and, in addition, are an absence away from attendance probation." He stops talking, as if waiting for me to jump in and defend myself, but really what could I possibly say. I have no good defense except that my brain gets so overwhelmed with what needs to get done each night, a light bulb with a wattage too bright, I fizzle into darkness and bite my lip till it bleeds. Or that sometimes sitting in class is akin to feeling the slow hand of death cover your face like a veil until it is all you can do not to get up and slit your wrists right there. Being in motion on the freeway, watching the buildings fold into the blur of other traffic speeding beside you, one hour until every artery is clogged, the last remnants of a care-free afternoon drive, get off the streets by three p.m. or rush hour will slow you down and your brain will scramble all over again—it's all you can do to deal, and even then wound tight in your chest, the anxiety ready to snap and uncoil.

"How are you feeling, Ms. Darling?" he asks.

"Feeling, sir?"

"About yourself."

"I feel fine, sir. I like school very much."

"Did you know Ms. Chang?"

"Did?" I ask, slightly panicked. Jesus Christ what did they do to her.

"I'm sorry, *do* you know Ms. Chang?"

I exhale. "Somewhat. A little, I dunno, I guess." For the love of fuck, these fucking people.

"Do you think you would consider yourself to be a young lady like Ms. Chang? Perhaps, in need of someone to speak with? We could arrange something on campus."

"Isn't that your job?"

"Oh!" he says perking up. "You would like someone to talk with? It can be arranged!"

"No, no I'm fine. I just, it's been a tough semester with auditions coming up. I'm trying out for the leads. What do you . . . do, Mr. Ingroff?"

"I facilitate healing."

"Oh."

"Will you work then to bring up your grades, show up for class? You'll need to if you're going to place first string."

"Sure," I answer.

"Good," he smiles, "a bright girl like you. It would be a shame to jeopardize your place here."

"What about me makes you think that I'm bright? You just said I'm failing."

"Only a feeling I get. Anyway, that's all. Please tell Corinne she can come in." And he lets me get away.

×

My mom is earth people. North American. Por vida, holmes. From La Junta, southern Colorado. SoCo. It's nothing fancy like Vail, it's in the southwest part, the part that spoons northern New Mexico. Prairies and plateaus. Tiny white and blue flowers that dot highways like bits of heaven. Jackrabbits leaping through the rainbow brush.

La Junta is a city that is most famous for being near another city: Trinidad. Fruits and fairies and fags, as the larger Republican Colorado population might say, or, the men-women, as my soft-spoken Mexican grandfather, my g-pa, my gampie, the man that rode in each Christmas on the Greyhound to the Pasadena train station with a bag of peanuts still in the shell, might say. Trinidad has Dr. Biber, the Wiz to the city's Oz, the first doctor in the US to perform gender reassignment surgery. His patients stay in town like Jesus's followers, and the truck drivers who roll in to fill up whistle and hoot as they pull away.

But La Junta is just where my grandpa dragged my grandma after the war. A chance to start over, where winter snow is shoveled by both white and brown hands and everyone in every gas station isn't a first cousin. Where alcoholism is present but not all-consuming. We are Nuevo Mexicanos. Wagon Mound and Ocate proud. Recipients of disenfranchisement, external and internalized racism, handed diseased blankets and shoved in the butt onto that Trail of Tears, tossed a bottle of liquid courage, rolling joints of trauma-coping mechanisms. My mother's ancestors crawled out of the red clay and left their handprints inside caves, stumbled off boats from Spain. They used the reflection off the stalagmites to light their way out of the past. They made arrows out of obsidian, carved homes into the cliffs, fire danced around a pit of burning shrubs underneath a navy, star-spotted sky, the white, chalky paint from their faces flaking off and floating into the wind. Animism and sage, a sacred circle undulating beneath a sun of life. The blood of our people deep in my veins, fortifying me through this bullshit, they whisper, *Mija keep going, mija do better.* Comanche Juan De Oñate. My red conquistador. Coyote. Split. Both and none. They were claimed for Spain, they were won by Mexico. They were sold in the Treaty of Guadalupe Hidalgo. They had their land snatched away, returned, and then challenged for the next two hundred years. They became *Yankees.* US "citizens" only when the US needed bodies to shoot full of holes in WWII and Vietnam. After that they were just brown bodies to be shot in the street like mangy dogs. They were called Indigenous. They were denied Native American rights and told they were Mestizo.

They wear cowboy hats, work the land, talk slow, call themselves rancheros, hang John F. Kennedy and Bobby Kennedy commemorative plates ordered from the back page of *Parade* magazine above the television. They nail them up next to Jesus and all his plastic flores. They have miniature enclosed dioramas in the front yard holding the

Mother. The essence. The miracle that was touched by the miracle. The woman.

They pull charcoaled cow heads out of the ground. They split the cabeza. They scoop the cheese. They leave oily fingerprints on the oilcloth. They sing me songs at night even when I'm alone in bed.

They say, *Mija you are not the impostor.*

×

Here's the thing though. It's all beautiful stuff but it's the wrong stuff. I'm in *Elay*, see? We're in Elay. There's no cheddar cheese and red and green Christmas chiles here. It's thin slices of lemon wedges on a paper plate. It's carne asada and carnitas and al pastor. It's a fucking fish taco, mang. No beans inside that burrito, no migas or breakfast tacos here. Chorizo or a taco de papa, that's what you get. Chopped white onions and cilantro. Here is spicy. Here is citrus infused. Corn tortillas, holmes. Get this flour shit away from me. Pulled in flapping from the ocean. Cindy Gallegos came over to dinner in the fifth grade. Her mom dropped her off. She asked if my mother had made Italian food when she pressed her fork into a plump enchilada and orange cheddar oozed out of the center.

No uvas.

Walkouts.

César Chávez.

Sleepy Lagoon murders.

Zoot Suit Riots.

Jaime Escalante, stand up and deliver, mi primo!
Pride.

It would be my luck not just to be half-Mexican, but the wrong kind of Mexican. I am not from East Los. My people are the borderlands, the frontera. I am a pale ghost of a bloody past. A daughter of the viceroyalty. A lady of Spain. But I'm not that either. I'm me. I'm SGV. I watch from the schoolyard as the sad boys mark up the EMF, throw down the emero. I live in the cool shadows of libraries. I cough and rip out pictures of Marlon Brando from old dusty biographies. I memorize the lines to *A Streetcar Named Desire*. I listen to Wanda Jackson and the Cramps inside my room at night, headphones resting around my neck turned full blast. I whisper *I have always depended on the kindness of strangers* as Vivien Leigh touches her own chest so lovingly, so delicately, as she realizes no one else will ever touch her that way again. In that moment of self-comfort there is strength. There is survival.

I am the girl who wonders what to say, if to say anything at all, when Amy Daniels, while standing in a group of girls that for some reason includes me, says, "Oh look, here comes Alex Molina and his entire family of beaners." I am the seven-year-old whose first-grade teacher announces, "Oh sweetie, your nanny's here," to which I reply, "That's my mommy."

I am tired of being your fly on the wall. Invisible bystander. A quiet barometer of how much is still wrong. You don't see me, but I see you. Pale and pretty on the outside, burned to a cinder in my soul.

×

Jessica Silverman is pulling out of the parking lot at school trying to hold a cigarette between her teeth and looking over her shoulder. We're listening to "Walking in LA" by Missing Persons and bobbing our heads in unison. The cigarette ashes on the console between us and she slams her foot on the brake and releases the wheel.

"Shit, shit!" she curses, brushing it away quickly with her hands. It falls onto my seat and she clenches her fists. "Motherfucking ash." She tries to rub it out of the black interior.

"Spit on your hand," I suggest.

She spits and wipes her palm, exposing well-manicured nails. A ripped-up friendship bracelet, a piece of black string, and large art-deco-style rings cling to her fingers and wrists like growths. I've never seen her without them and I can tell they've been showered many times. I shake my head at the ever-expanding spit spot near my thigh that she is feverishly rubbing, probably because she's stoned. The ash is long gone, was never a problem, the seats are leather, but I don't say anything and look out the window. In the rearview Dan Meanstreetz Martínez is rolling up on his skateboard. He's wearing his usual ragtag garbage pail of shreds. Punk patches pinned to black jeans, a crumbling denim jacket that smells like armpits, rusted studs around the elbows. A giant Nausea patch the size of his entire back, pinned to his ass, hangs down like a thin delicate train.

Jessica's foot is off the brake and we roll backward as Battle of the Ash continues.

"Watch out!" I shout. She looks up and screams.

"Fucking bitches!" yells Meanstreetz, slamming his hands on the back of Jessica's mom's Mercedes.

She shoves her foot down, pulls the parking brake, and we both spin around in our seats and onto our knees, peeking over the top of the leather like kids at the banister on Christmas morning. I hold my breath and so does Jessica. "It was Meanstreetz," I whisper.

"Should we get out? I mean, did we hit him?"

I nod. "I think so." Smoke is rising from the bottom of the floor near Jessica's feet.

"Oh Jesus!" I shriek, covering my mouth with one hand and pointing at the smoke with the other. I back into the window, legs beneath me.

"Fucking fuck!" she yells, leaning down and looking for the cigarette.

Her door swings open and Dan glares at us, all *Redrum, Here's Johnny*–looking and we scream again. "What the fuck, you fucking graveyard brains!" He reaches in and grabs us by the shoulders. We raise our hands to our faces shrieking and jump in our seats.

"I dropped a cigarette!" she says panicked, kneels down, and resumes searching the floor for it.

"Get out!" he shouts again.

"I can't you caveman! Can't you see I'm fer-reaking?"

"You fucking hit me, bitch, with your tank!"

"Oh, she did not," I say, opening my door and walking

to her side of the car. I crouch beside her. "It's underneath the seat."

"Don't you think I know that, Inspector Gadget?" she says, raising her head and getting snappy with me.

"Ugh, it smells like skunk in here. Move." He yanks her by the arm and she stumbles out of the car. Dan rolls the seat back and grabs the smoking culprit. "You burned a hole in the carpet. Smooth move, Einstein."

"Goddamnit!" she says, clenching her fists and stamping her foot. "My fucking mom is going to kill me."

"She'll never know unless you tell her. Roll the seat back, air this dump truck out, and you're fine."

"Let me buy you pancakes," she says taking a giant breath.

I kneel on the hood and shield my eyes. "We were heading to IHOP. I'll throw down on fries."

Dan looks up the long set of stairs heading to King Hall and then at us. "You've got Lavoi, what did you guys do today?" he asks, looking at me.

"First chapter of *Beloved*. If you haven't read it don't bother going."

"I need to go to my locker first."

"Why?" she asks, pushing in the car lighter and pulling a pack of smokes from the front pocket of her backpack.

"Homework."

"We're coming back for Arts. Two hours, tops."

He looks at his Swatch and thinks.

"As a thank-you and an apology for almost hitting you," she offers.

"For hitting me," he says, opening the backseat and throwing his skateboard in. "You hit me, bitch, no almost."

"There is no try," I say, taking the cigarette from her mouth and sucking a drag. Dan squints up his face and looks old, serene, taps his fingertips together like Yoda. *"Only do,"* we finish in unison.

×

We're at the IHOP on Fremont, right before Valley, and Dan is dipping fries into Tabasco and making hot sauce art across the plate. A smiley face, a pentagram, a shooting star.

"Saw you scamming on Lydi last weekend at Jaime's party."

He raises an eyebrow at me and takes a fry bite, sticks out his tongue, and lets fry mush fall on the table. "No te metas en mis asuntos, puta."

"I don't even know what that means," I say, rolling my eyes.

"Surprise, surprise, Darling," he says, flipping me off.

"Oh please, are we going to do this?" asks Jessica, leaning forward, about to shove a forkful of pancakes in her mouth. "Can I be invited to the conversation? Please? I only paid for lunch, I don't feel like paying for a Spanish to English translator too."

"How extremely unracist of you, Jessie." He takes a pancake off her stack, rolls it up, and shoves it in his mouth.

"You're so rude."

He screws up his face and mimics me silently, limp wrist smacking his hand against his chest.

"It's actually unbelievable how offensive you are."

He smiles and ketchup drools from the sides of his mouth.

"What the fuck, asshole?" Jessica says, setting her fork down. "You're such a fucking pig."

He snorts and little bits of pancake shoot out of his mouth and into the air. "You love it." He chokes, his cheeks full.

The thing is, Dan is half-right. Everybody does love it. He is undisputedly gorgeous, completely nihilistic, and super easy to fuck. A dynamo recipe if there ever was one. Dark eyes, wavy shiny black hair, scruff, a nose that makes him look like a Mayan god. High cheekbones and dimples, white teeth, and the most beautiful, heartbreaking smile. He is a megababe. It doesn't work on me though, because he's also a pig. He lurches forward at Jessica and snorts.

"You should bottle your essence and sell it. You can call it Eau de Man Slut," I say.

"Eau de Garbage Disposal is more like it," she sneers. "Seriously, you smell disgusting. When was the last time you showered?"

"I slept in Venice last night."

"Shut. Up." I roll my eyes.

"I did. Swear to god. Sam and I were skating and passed out in Muscle Park. Woke up with the sunrise and some nasty seagull pecking at my nuts."

"Probably because you smell like a rotting corpse," says Jessica, her attentions reabsorbed in the pancake pile.

"I don't believe you," I say, sticking my fork into hash browns. "How'd you even get out there? I know I didn't take you."

"I have my own wheels, *dude*."

"Bullshit."

"I do. My dad got me a Honda last month. '87 hatchback. It's pretty mint. Don't need you rolling up in your mom's Aerostar, thanks."

"Well, now I know why I haven't seen you in forever."

He looks down at his fries and doesn't say anything.

"I heard you fucked Chloe. If we're still talking about the brain-dead," chimes Jessica, scanning the syrups. She picks up the hot-pink boysenberry.

Dan makes the kind of face that says, *Come on, man*, but then says something else instead. "She's nice."

"You don't have to tell me. She's my best friend, remember?"

"Yeah, some best friend. Fuck, girls are ruthless."

"Oh, and what?" I ask, shoving ketchuped hash browns into my mouth. "Guys are so thoughtful?"

"Yeah. We are. We can be."

"Oh, sure." I eye roll.

"Join the gender revolution, pig breath," huffs Jessica. "Maybe you've heard of it, a little thing called women's rights? Little piece of radical law called the ERA?"

"Don't tell me about shit I already know."

"Yeah," I add, "why don't you buy a Bikini Kill record or something?"

"Because it's 1996, dummy, and I like Massive Attack."

"Why don't you huff paint with some Jerry's kids since you're all *der*."

"Why don't you suck a Fruit Roll-Up off my butthole."

"Why don't you get AIDS and die?"

"Why don't you accept a gift from Whoville so your heart can grow three sizes?"

"Why don't you choke on a shark dick and drown?"

"It's a whale dick, estúpida. You fucked it up."

"Why don't you two hump and get it over with?" says Jessica, pouring hot-pink syrup on her pancakes. Dan grabs her sausage and shoves it in his mouth, chewing like the abovementioned pig, for our amusement.

"I would but I don't want scabies," I shoot back.

Dan looks up at me and he doesn't look fun anymore, he looks red, blushed, worried. All his good-time energies have seeped out around him and Jessica and I glance at each other.

"You okay?" she asks.

"Yeah," he says scooting out of the booth. "Gotta take a shit."

"Eww." She throws a napkin at him. "You really are a hog."

"Hakuna matata," he grins, waving his arms back and forth.

An old couple sits behind us in the next booth and the old man looks up and says something to Dan.

"What?" he asks, turning and looking at the old man.

"Mijo," he says, pointing a shaky finger at the ground. "You dropped your glasses."

Dan looks down. His glasses case lies beside the booth near the open lip of his backpack. "Gracias," he says, nodding at the old man wearing old-man clothes that make me want to close my eyes. I don't want to think about the grandparents I never call. Or the thought of them dying. Dan reaches down and grabs his glasses, shoves them in his pocket. "Gracias, gracias."

The old man nods and smiles turning back to his wife. "Ofelia," he says, holding out his arm for a napkin. She pulls one from the dispenser and hands it to him. Outside the window large wooden scaffolding has been placed around the massive open lot across from the Toys"R"Us and Ocean Star dim sum banquet hall. A giant sign advertising something called the Fremont Commons is stapled to one of the wooden boards. It's been tagged and wheat postered. EMF is spray-painted on top of a wrinkled, dripping cartoon of Pete Wilson. Inside the site a huge yellow tractor cranes its neck and shovels large chunks of dirt and cement. I wonder who the hell thought to develop all this backland. All this in-between. This plot of dirt by the police car parking lot and the 1950s paper manufacturer. The longest, flattest stretch of nothing green this side of Huntington Boulevard. Dan comes back from the bathroom, bobbing along. He slides back in and smiles.

"Ahhhh," he says, as if he just took a sip of something fizzy and delicious.

"Well I'm not hungry anymore," says Jessica, dropping her fork.

"Yeah," I echo. "Dit-to."

She wipes her mouth with a napkin and tosses it on the table, defeated. "You think looking like that gives you license to be a dick, but it doesn't, hog brain. You won't look like that forever."

He stares at me and grabs a handful of hash browns and shoves them in his mouth, bits of ketchupy potato on his fingertips. "Me so pretty."

"I hate you," she says, her eyes watering, and just then something registers that hadn't registered before. They've fucked, and he left. I look at her face, puffy and sad.

"Well then go home, Jessica, because I'm just getting started."

×

I make my way up our street from the bus stop around the corner. Mom's car is in the driveway. I walk inside, drop my bag on the table. The kitchen is empty. I follow her voice into the master bedroom, where she's on the phone. She sees me, waves me away, and turns her body toward the wall.

"Well honey, if he's, well, stop interrupting, just listen, if he's doing it now, it won't change, you can't argue a man out of that behavior. Please believe, Lyla. Lyla, stop talking and let me finish."

"Momma," I say, flopping on the bed. I raise my arm

toward her, touch her hand, she pushes it away and mouths, *Stop*.

"Mommy," I say again, and nudge closer.

"Lyla, hold on, no, just wait, hold on." She covers the receiver with a hand and looks at me, bothered, "What is it?"

"I'm hungry."

"I brought sushi from work, it's Bristol Farms. It's in the fridge." She uncovers the phone and starts again.

"Lyla, if you feel this way why did you move in with him? See, this is why you don't move in with every Tom, Dick, and asshole."

I sit up and nudge closer. "Momma," I repeat. Except this time she's had it and her eyes mean business. I start to scramble away but it's too late.

"What is it?" she shrieks, still wielding the phone in one hand. "You're like an incessant pest buzzing in my ear! *Mommy, mommy, mommy*, can't you see I'm on the goddamned phone with your sister?"

I take a deep breath, push the air in a circle through my stomach, making it do cartwheels before I breathe it out again. I want to watch movies in her bed. I want to rest my head in her lap. I transform my breath and exhale a *whatever*.

"Can I take the photo basket in my room?"

"Jesus Christ, Nicole. Fine, take it. Can I talk with your sister, please, is that okay with you? Shut the door." She picks up the receiver a final time. "I'm sorry, honey, your sister's whining at me. What I'm saying is it isn't going to change, the thing you need to get through your head, honey, he's an abuser and if he's hit you once, he'll hit you again. Christ, don't you have a girlfriend you can stay with?"

×

That night lying in bed, I think about Claire. The cool white shadow of the moon moving across my wall. The jalousie windows with their many slats cast dark noirish shadows in its spotlight. I could get up and be a moonlight marionette. Like the porcelain masks with the painted tears in my sister's high school bedroom before she left.

Claire looking over her shoulder while in line at the campus coffee shop, talking to me out of nowhere. I looked around to make sure I was the one she was talking to. "I mean, fuck everyone. Fuck this place, fuck you." She huffed and checked her watch. "What is taking this bitch so long?" The girl in front of us was fishing through her purse, lip gloss and receipts falling to the ground. Claire groaned. I gulped and could feel the five-dollar bill sweaty in my palm. "It's like this entire place is just an idiot factory and—" and before she could finish the barista at the window of our little A-frame coffee shop poked her head out of the vestibule and called, "Next!" I hung back, desperate, waiting for Claire to finish ordering and complete her thought, but instead she took a deep gulp, flipped her hair, pulled her Wayfarers down, and stalked off. An angry cloud of psychic beauty. Iced coffee: black.

Claire stealing magazines from the campus bookstore. A place the high schoolers weren't even allowed to be. But she went in there all the time, without remorse, without shame. I'd watch her waltz in, scoop up an *LA Weekly* and a *Rolling Stone* or whatever, flip her hair over her shoulder, and confidently waltz back out. Sometimes spitting when she left. She was such a marvel, a character from some teenage movie crossed over into this universe and sprinkled generously over our lives, except everyone was a stupid pod person and had no idea how lucky we were to walk alongside her.

I try to imagine her in a girls' home. Can she stomp there like an angry dinosaur? Can she burn a hole in your head with a death-ray stare? Can she dismiss you with the turn of her head? Can she see inside you to the shitty piece of shit coward that you probably are? Can she make you convulse with her clarity? Float and vibrate, tremble and fly? Can she, you know, use the pay phone?

×

Later that week at the Malahini, the Whittier motel where the punk kids rent a room every couple of weeks to throw dog pile beer bong ragers, I find myself sitting leaned against the bathroom door nursing the champagne of beers, a slow moan emanating from beneath. My foot touches the orange-black, gum-spotted carpet. I can hear the soft panting and whining of a girl. It's quiet like a pigeon, a small, rolling, high-pitched purr. After a few minutes of silence the door swings open and I'm pushed forward. The 40 slips between my fingers and rolls onto its side. Thick, foaming streams of beer seep into this dirty merkin called a floor covering.

"Come on," says Dan, zipping his fly. He reaches down and grabs my arm.

"Hey!" I shout. "What the fuck?"

"Time to go. Come on."

I scramble to my feet and brush the dirty Malahini Motel off my butt. I spin in the direction of the fallen and she's sitting there at the edge of the toilet seat, her eyes all sad and sad looking. She's naked. Of course. *Of course.* All broken up and stupid fucking sad. She doesn't even go to school with us. I don't even know who this sad sack is. Hair all drippy and stringy in her pretty, dewy face. She looks up at me, covers her face, and starts to cry. Some blond. Come on, I want to say, come the fuck on, what did you expect? I shake my head at her as Dan pulls me toward the door. Really. *Really?* Don't look sad. Don't look *sad.* Jesus.

"Puta, move it!" He shoves me down the lava-rock-sided stairs toward the empty parking lot.

"Who was that?"

"Who cares."

"Well, I do."

"Just get in," he says, shoving his keys into his new old hatchback. He leans across the seat and pops my lock. "I want some fucking Noodle Planet."

"Is it all-night?"

"Think so."

"Who was that girl?"

"She goes to PHS, she hangs out."

"With who?"

"Oh my god. With me and Mikey and Arturo and Bennie. Chill out. She's into skaters. She's nice."

"She didn't look nice. She looked naked."

"Come on Nikki, chill."

"How many girls have you slept with?"

"I don't know, like ten. Maybe more, I don't know."

"So I have to leave a party because you just fucked your good friend, Naked Girl?"

"She started crying. Cut me a break."

"Why?"

"I don't know. I just don't want to see a girl cry."

"Oh my god. So you run out? You don't even, like, talk to her? Was she a virgin?"

"Jesus, I don't know. Look, you wanna stay? Cos you can find your own way home from Whittier. It's okay by me."

"Can you even drive? You look drunk."

"I'm always drunk."

I don't say anything and look out the window as the car rumbles to life. He backs out and pulls into the wide street.

"That party was bogus anyway." He squeezes his nose and snorts. Oh Jesus, he's high.

"I fail to see how that party was bogus. Jessica's not even here yet. It's only eleven."

"Ugh, Jessica is the last person I want to see. Come on, let's go."

"You mind-voodooed another girl into catching the scabies. You're such a slave to the vagine, I swear."

"It just sucked is all."

"You're such an elevator operator."

"Oh yeah?" he says, pulling onto Whittier Boulevard. "And what kind of wild time were you having on the floor, listening to me bone?"

"You just masturbate inside them."

"She called me *gorgeous*. No one's called me that before."

"Oh geez. Get over yourself." I look out the window as we pull onto the 57 and the giant cement soundproof walls rise around us. The small blue, green, pink 1960s stucco homes that line the freeway, old beaters, and broken rusted swing sets in yellow yards, fade below. A copper rolls onto the freeway behind us and I see Dan look nervously in the rearview mirror and swallow. "Relax, we're kids. He's not after us."

"Oh, isn't he?"

The cop picks up and zooms past. His lights switch on and his siren bleats. He speeds into the distance, toward some primer fitted seventies Chevelle.

"See? He's only working the holmes trail tonight."

Dan pushes the lighter in. "Hey, dame uno," and wiggles his fingers for a cigarette. I lean down and unzip the front pocket of his backpack and grab two.

"Promise me you'll never buy rollies."

"Maybe I should." The lighter pops and he sparks up. "Maybe then you wouldn't bum me dry all the time." I roll my eyes. "Tell me, Nik." He takes a drag and blows it sideways out of his mouth, like some sexy black-and-white Rudolph Valentino. "Do you think I'm good-looking?"

I shift nervously in my seat and let out a little whatever-dude snort.

"No really. I'm curious."

"Come on, you just had sex with some *blond* chick," I say, taking my own drag. I look out the window and then back at him. He's still looking at me, waiting for an answer.

"No really, I want to know."

"Jesus, that girl's warm burger wasn't warm enough? Your dick cheese is probably mutating on her as we speak and you need your friends to kiss it, too?"

"Why can't you answer me?"

"Why's it important?"

"It's not. I'm just curious."

"What schizophrenic told you you were worthless and priceless at the same time?"

"My mother."

"Fine. Do you think I'm pretty?"

"Sure. You're cute. Real cute."

"Huh." The Miller brewery is on our right and I look out the window, the smell of the duck farm behind us sending poo stench in through the AC vents. The warm smell of hops makes my stomach turn.

"God it's just so stupid I don't know why you need me to tell you. I mean, obviously. Duh. Helen Keller could, like, tell you that." I blow smoke out the rolled-down window and cross my free arm over my chest. "You're such an asshole." He leans forward and turns on the radio. It's Alice in Chains. Layne Staley is all, *Can't kill the rooster.* Who even is the goddamn rooster to begin with? I never know. "What is this dorky song even about?" I say finally, stubbing my smoke out in the ashtray.

"His dad."

"What?"

"The song. His dad was in Vietnam. His dad is Rooster."

I'm quiet, watch as the lights of Duarte and East Pasadena start to show themselves in the distance. The new-fangled, old-fashioned, resort-style Spaghetti Factory, where the hardworking Azusa Mexican moms and pops bring their kids on special dinner nights, has a line of cars trying to get into the parking lot. "Well it's a solid jam. I'll give it that."

He laughs. "You're so weird."

"You're so weird."

"Why are you so dick hungry for Mike Pinedo? He's gay, you know that, right?"

"Of course I know that. I'm not stupid. And I'm not dick hungry for anyone."

"Sure you are."

"This conversation is officially prehistoric."

"Come on, you moon all over him."

"When are you watching me moon over people?"

"So what then, you're just never having sex?"

"Jesus. I don't know. Yeah. One day."

"Don't you think about it?"

I turn and swing in his direction, lay a fat one on his thigh. He pulls his face into an outraged grimace. "Fuck you."

"Fuck you, leave me alone," I say.

"I just don't get what your deal is."

"Look, not everyone has that adorable nihilism you pass around like AIDS. Okay? I care about shit."

"It's a piece of skin."

"It's a membrane."

"Exactly."

"You're a fucking idiot. You don't even get it."

"Yeah, that's the point. I don't."

"So then what? You want us to fuck? Is that it?" I feel all the blood rush into my cheeks and look out the window as the city buildings and hotels roll by. The mall. The bright lights of commerce. Oh to be inside the mall, the sweet, sweet mall. I feel myself aging in fast-forward like a 1950s life-science film documenting animal decay. Carrion. Carry me. Or maybe that one about the atomic bomb. Chewing and snapping gum, stoned, the world exploding from a projector screen onto a smudged chalkboard. Black-and-white mushroom cloud of foxhole faith. Jesus help us all. Father, Mother, keep us safe. In the blink of an X-ray eye it's gone. Good I don't give a shit. I had a paper due next week anyway. Seriously, *who fucking cares? BLOW IT UP.*

I've said it now, said the thing he was waiting for. Like a detective playing cat and mouse, changing the subject, shooting the shit. He teased it out of me, tricked me into his evil submission just to prove that I'm not as special as I put on. I'm not immune to his DNA, no matter how much I pretend otherwise. He wanted to let me know that he knew. It's all a game to him. I'm like everyone else, under his dirty thumb.

He laughs. "You and me, fuck? Yeah. You wish."

×

Sarah leans in, the biggest shit-eating grin plastered across her face, and gives me a nudge in the ribs. "What?" I whine, shooing her away.

"Dude, dude," she mumbles, giggling, "you faded?"

"Yeah," I nod, "trying to be." I push her arm and she sits forward and punches the wooden theater seats in front of us.

"Stop it!" I say, and pull her back. "Lie down!"

"Man!" she yells. A young couple sitting up front turns and looks at us.

"Come on," I say, irritated, "shut up." Except for the couple, the Laserium is pretty empty, two or three kids, probably also ditching, slouch alone in the corners of the theater, most likely masturbating or getting high. Sarah shakes her head, reaches under her butt and pulls out a pack of smokes, "Here." I take one and she lights us up. The couple up front is smoking a joint.

"It smells like a skunk's asshole," I say.

"Hey, man, check *it out*!" She points with her cigarette

at the rainbow swirl above us, like I can't see, like I don't have the same psychedelic trip happening right in front of me. The end of her cigarette glows red and I pull her arm down. Being with Sarah feels familiar and comfortable, especially after the last semester of trailing behind Chelo.

"Don't! You'll get us in trouble."

"Pfft, shit, like he cares, that dude's stoneder than we are," she says referring to the laserist. Each show is live and performed by some leftover, baked Floyd-head from Van Nuys, flicking buttons and levers and magic at our ojos.

"Whatever, we don't have to, like, go flaunting it in his face, he could call the cops."

"You are so *tripped out!*" she sputters, nodding her head vigorously to the "Brain Damage" riff. She air drums the seats in front and I pull her back down. "Man, you're like cheesy *Up in Smoke* tripped out right now. His name's Raaaaalph!" she says quoting the movie and waving her tongue all over the place.

And that's too much, that's it for me and I crack up, kicking the seat in front and covering my mouth to keep it all stuffed inside. I look over at her and she's playing little invisible drumsticks, twisting her face all up into a Nick Mason grimace and then on cue with the music puts the sticks down, picks up an invisible mic and opens her mouth, seamlessly transforming into David Gilmour as the song transitions into "Eclipse," *All that you eat and everyone you meet, all that you slight and everyone you fight. All that is now, all that is gone, all that's to come and everything under the sun is in tune but the sun is eclipsed by the moooooooooon.*

I squeal, tears running down my face, pound my feet on the floor, and Sarah just rolls back and forth like she's in pain, holding on to her sides. I see one of the boys sitting alone on the other end of the theater sit up nervously. "Look, look," I wheeze, pointing at him. "He zipped his fly!" Sarah pounds her feet and squeals. The boy stands quickly and walks toward the theater exit. A rush of light floods long cracks that run across the room and over the light show, making it ripple, escaping back into the outdoors when the door swings shut.

"Girls," says the laserist's deep voice, "girls, that's enough."

"Oh shit!" Sarah grabs my hand and we bolt up, jumping over wooden seats and stumbling as we hurry. We tear and heave, running toward the double doors and explode into the lobby. I trip, laughing, Sarah already halfway toward the exit. I stand up and run after her even though at this point it doesn't matter, the observatory is empty, even the information booth is abandoned. I pause in the rotunda and look up at the sky murals, faded and water stained like some LA interpretation of the Sistine Chapel—the hand of man touching the hand of science, the stars and moon, the blue night sky waiting in the distance, but man, man pushes on. I look down at the huge gold swinging pendulum measuring the earth's gravitational pull. Back and forth. There is a Styrofoam fast food cup sitting at the bottom. Sarah appears in the entrance of the observatory, leans against the giant green copper door and looks at me, "Come on," she says, trying to catch her breath, "let's go."

In the lawn out front we lie on our backs. Behind us the Hollywood sign, in front the old, beautiful art deco masterpiece, to the right, a bust of James Dean and an honorary plaque placed for him, to celebrate the fight scene in *Rebel Without a Cause* that was filmed right here. I think about Natalie Wood floating to the bottom of the ocean, hands above her head, neck back like some Hollywood Ophelia. I tug at the grass as my high subsides. I feel sleepy and warm; to the left, the horizon; everything. "It's so beautiful," I whisper.

"What?" asks Sarah, grabbing handfuls of grass and letting them blow behind us in the wind.

"The building, it's old. A famous architect built it, I forget his name."

Sarah sits up and squints at the building, its white and copper green domes. "How do you know?" She tilts her head and takes it in.

"My dad told me." I sit up, too. "Hey, do you have more smokes?"

"Sure." She pulls them out and we light up. "Lookit, it's that guy from inside."

"Oh yeah?"

"Yeah. Where do you think he goes?"

"Eww, who cares? He was yanking it in the planetarium."

Sarah shrugs and exhales. "Meh."

"You know, dork butt, it isn't actually 1977, Jerry Garcia isn't, like, sitting over there waiting for you to, like, I don't know, talk to him. That's probably some Nirvana nutsack who smells bad."

"Since when don't you like Nirvana?"

"Like forever, they're sexist and stuff."

Sarah rolls her eyes. "Did Consuelo Medina tell you that?"

"No. I'm allowed to not like Nirvana on my own."

"Oh, I'm sorry, I forgot, Consuelo is punk rock. Jessica Silverman told you Nirvana sucks. So, what, are you, like, a riot grrrl now? You're, like, three years too late, by the way." She stubs out her cigarette and stands.

"You're the second stupid person to point that out to me this week. I know when riot grrrl happened, okay?"

"God, *stupid*?! Are you serious? You just called me *stupid*? When did you become such a nasty jerk? Like, how can you talk to me like that?"

"Geez, I'm sorry." But she's already heading across the lawn. "Where are you going?" I call, jumping to my feet.

"To fuck Jerry."

"You're nuts."

"And you're a virgin. Take the bus home without me. Love you!"

"Wait, really?" I say, jogging to catch up. "I thought we were going to Oki Dog!" She turns around and smiles, waves and blows a kiss then kneels in front of Jerry, who on closer inspection, is not that bad looking, if you like a seventies stoner type of eighteen-year-old dude. I stop and look behind me. "Well, shit, thanks!" I shout, but they're talking already and he's getting up and she's flipping her hair and laughing. It's like some stupid after-school special with Scott Baio, like *Stoned* or something. "Ugh, seriously!?" I call one more time, to myself and I guess no one. I check my watch, three thirty, turn around and start the walk back down the hill toward Los Feliz and Western.

×

Elizabeth Taylor holds a small bouquet and nods, smiling, she says, "Gracias, gracias." Rock stands back looking sort of mortified and embarrassed, "Leslie," he admonishes, trying not to assert too strong a hand over his new, lovely, enthusiastic bride. But Elizabeth doesn't hear him; well, she does, but she doesn't care and marches on in all her philanthropic glory. In all her beauty and openhearted goodness. "What are your names?" she asks the two chubby Mexicans, mother and daughter, clothed in beige, earth-colored cotton work skirts. They nod cautiously at her eager kindness. They glance at one another and then at Rock. "Lupe," answers the mother, holding Elizabeth's suitcase. "Beta," answers Lupe's daughter.

"Lupe? Beta?" asks Elizabeth, still feeling generous.

"Sí, señora," they chirp in unison, nodding and kow-towing like Marlon Brando in *The Teahouse of the August Moon*.

"Gracias, Lupe," offers Elizabeth, still not finished.

She gives a final grateful nod, practically a bow, and they scurry away. Rock's eyes almost pop out of his head.

"Don't be so nice to the Mexicans," clucks Rock, "they're, like, savages and stuff."

"I wasn't aware graciousness was out of practice," she answers back. "I'm still me."

"You're my wife, woman," he says, trying to put a blanket on her fire.

"I still have a mind," she answers, shaking her head.

I mean, really Rock. It's Elizabeth for god's sake. All your other damsels will pretend you weren't a homo after you die. Will tell newspapers it was a bad blood transfusion. They'll mitigate the real tragedy, the silent killer in desperate need of attention and offer an MGM explanation. Your precious Doris Day, who even in the end felt she had to protect you from your own awful hedonism, kept your secret to the grave. She understood you just couldn't *help yourself*. Right. Only Elizabeth will stand up in front of Ronald Reagan, her middle finger extended and say, *Yeah? So what? So the hell what? And who here doesn't like to fuck?*

Oh Lupe, you sad brown-eyed-cow thing. I wish I could go back in time and dump a bucket of ice water on George Stevens's head. But now, here, where you are trapped forever on celluloid, I love you with a fiery passion and wonder who you were in real life, the way I wonder how many extras in silent films lie dead inside their caskets at Hollywood Forever and how many are laying flowers there instead.

Mom walks out of the bathroom putting earrings on and scans the room for a wayward sneaker. I burp teriyaki and suck the last of my Oki Orange Bang and shake the cup for remnants. She has to work today even though it's her day off. The wedding she designed the night before was postponed till this evening and now all the arrangements have wilted. "How many times can you watch that thing?" she asks, shaking her head.

"As many times as I want," I answer, kicking my feet up where I lie on her queen-size bed.

"I have to take it back tonight," she says, grabbing her green flower apron, throwing it over her head, and fastening it at her back. She spies the shoe behind the dresser, shoves her foot into it.

"That's fine."

Mom doesn't like Elizabeth Taylor movies because in the sixties she looked like Elizabeth Taylor. A brown Elizabeth Taylor. Same eyes, same hair, same mouth, same face shape. People used to tell her that while she stood in line at the grocery store or while she was waiting tables in Houston. Mom always says Elizabeth has a fat neck and no legs. Mom also doesn't appreciate when I tell her I love Elizabeth Taylor because she looks like the photos I've seen of her when she was younger. She always rolls her eyes. *Uh-huh*, she'll say, because she knows that's mostly full of shit. I don't like Elizabeth Taylor because she looks like my mom, I like Elizabeth Taylor because she's glamorous, beautiful, and dramatic.

I will name my children Elizabeth and Elvis. They will have black wet hair and beautiful violet eyes and voices like angels. Mom likes Bob Marley and the Wailers, Los Lobos, Joni Mitchell, Paul Simon, Cat Stevens. She's always humming that Ladysmith Black Mambazo song. Mom was a hippie. Came to California on a Greyhound, nibbling tamales she brought inside her purse to not pass out from hunger, got off in Half Moon Bay. She hates the fifties, can't stomach the early sixties. She's all about, "My thirties were the best years of my life." *Uh-huh*, I'll say, knowing full well that's a crock of cat food. I was born when she was in her thirties, and that's when dad slinked out of state never to show his face again. That's when my sister got married at nineteen and decided enough was enough with our trashy horseshit family, only to marry into a backwoods PCP family somehow trashier than ours. They might as well have raised their kids inside the stumps of the redwoods that lined their property, they were so much like wolves. And that's saying a lot, seeing that Mom and Dad dragged Lyla up and down the United States in a VW van, living in communes like cheesy characters from *Forrest Gump*. Mom's thirties are when we became, well, Mom and I, and I know firsthand that transition was hard.

"I'm going to be in Beverly Hills till around midnight. Can you take the bus to the Blockbuster? I need the car," she says doing that thing where she ignores what I've said. *It's not that I don't love you honey, it's just that I don't care.*

"Can't we just pay the late fee?"

"It's already late."

"It's getting dark out and I just started it."

"You've seen it a hundred times."

"Not a hundred. Five."

"That's four more times than you need to see it. Please, Nicole, I'm tired and running late. Either I take it now or you take it later."

"I already took the bus all the way from Hollywood."

She stops and looks at me. "What were you doing in Hollywood?"

"Nothing, fine, I'll take it."

"Thank you." She pulls a twenty from her purse and hands it over. "Get yourself dinner and be in bed when I get home."

"It's Friday."

"It's Thursday."

"God, I'm sixteen."

"You keep reminding me. Be in bed."

"No."

"Nicole."

"Fine whatever."

"Don't *whatever* me. I can't afford to put you in summer school. You're too old to act like this."

"I didn't say anything."

"One more letter in the mail and it's serious trouble this time. Deep-shit trouble."

"Oh yeah, I'm really scared," I say, mocking her.

"Don't test me and don't smoke cigarettes in my house."

"I don't. I smoke them outside. And it's dad's house."
As soon as I say it I want to snatch it back.

"Don't smoke them!" she says slamming her arm down on the dresser, her loose jewelry rattles and the mirror shakes. "Goddamnit!"

"Okay, okay, I'm just kidding. Relax."

"I'm not kidding," she says, her voice getting tight and twisted like it's getting pinched around the edges. "Please," she says, looking up. "And it's your grandfather's house. Your father doesn't own so much as a comb."

"Okay, chill. I wasn't going out tonight anyway. I just want to watch *Giant*."

"I'm tired," she says finally.

"I know, okay? I get it."

"I wish you did."

×

Mike is sitting on his mattress unfolding a small square of tinfoil. Inside sits a sticky, caked-together yellow clump of powder. I dropped off the movie and took the bus to Whittier. Tweak. He sets the tinfoil on a 1970s thrift store copy of a *National Geographic* photography book about flowers, and cuts roughly. I don't ask and he doesn't offer. He leans down, covers one nostril, and snorts, closes his eyes, leans back, and shakes his head, flops it forward and snorts again. Dan is so full of horseshit and seagull rabies. I don't moon all over Mike. I just love his company and well, if

I moon over Mike then I also moon over Dan and Dan is a hog. Two wrongs don't make a left. Hypothesis wrong.

Mike's aquamarine eyes open and he looks like a zonked dog. A sleepy-eyed, gorgeous dog. His lips part and I see his tongue resting inside like a fat sponge. His bare chest is sweaty and he wipes an open palm across it as he stands and walks to the metal clothing rack that his vintage Kramer shirts hang on. An overstuffed olive green 1950s armchair holds the remainder of his attire.

"How come you sleep out here?" I ask, looking around the small garage. He's invited me over a bunch of times before but this is the first time I've taken him up on the offer. Christmas twinkle lights hang around the room, there's a vintage Playskool record player, and different postcards—James Dean from *Giant*, two pink marshmallow Peeps on fire, and John Waters, most likely ripped from the postcard rack at Penny Lane or Tower—are thumbtacked to the wall. His own giant oil painting hangs above the mattress: Dorothy's head floating over Sally Bowles, Toto in hand, looking off hopeful together into the nothing, Sally straddling that chair, black bowler hat held defiantly above her head. A 1940s gay pinup of a naked blindfolded man in business socks with a black tie wrapped around his wrists, holding back his arms, hangs next to it. It's been ripped out of an old beefcake catalog and I wonder what life it's had, to make its way here, to 1996 La Puente, California, belonging to the half-white, half-brown answer to the question, What is the most beautiful thing alive on two legs? In the corner of the photograph, the shadow of another man looms forebodingly. Mike tells me it's a Bob Mizer. Whoever that is.

"Marta," he says, meaning his stepmother, "won't let me in the house," finally answering after a long silence. "She thinks I'll give the toilet seat AIDS and kill my sisters." He snorts again and swallows phlegm. "And who knows?" he asks smiling. He gives a lazy laugh and bobs his head.

"Who knows what?"

"Who knows?" He stands and walks to an unfinished painting of Elizabeth Taylor in profile. "Here," he says, handing it over and pulling a pack of smokes off his table. He pulls one out with his fat, long brown fingers and lights up with a lighter that magically materializes from his boxer shorts. He grins at me from under a flop of sandy brown beach hair, his brown face stubble pulling into dimples.

"For me?"

"Yeah. You said you liked *Butterfield 8*, that means you're a real fan."

"But it's not even my birthday or anything."

He snorts again and his eyes relax into half slits. He wipes his hand messily across his mouth. "When's your birthday?"

"Not for, like, I dunno, six months."

"Then happy half birthday. You can't have it yet though, it isn't finished."

"Okay, sure," I say handing it back. "Cool, thank you."

"De nada."

"It's beautiful. I love it."

His feet are brown and long, the toes wide and slender all at the same time. I have never noticed a man's feet before and looking at his feet now, at the golden, sun-bleached hair around the ankles, I am struck by their beauty. His surfboard sits on the floor near the mattress and he shoves it with his foot and flips his hair again and smiles, nodding at me. I smile too, but I have no idea why.

"Cool," he whispers. He snorts and swallows more phlegm. "Oh, hey," he lays the painting back down on top of a stack of other stretched canvases. "I'll need it for class in a few weeks but that's it. Gotta show Mr. Gotto and then it's yours."

"Sure, whatever."

"Cool." He sits back down next to me, and smiles. "Hey, let's smoke a J, yeah?"

"Yeah, totally."

"Cool. Can you roll?"

"Sure."

"Okay, I'm gonna go inside and get some orange juice before they come home. The weed is in that box over there. Cool?"

"Coolness."

"Cool." He stops in his doorway and looks back at me. "Hey."

"Yeah?"

"Hey yeah," he nods again as if listening to some music only he can hear. There is a long silence and his eyes glaze over as he looks past my head, a slow strange smile spreads across his face until his eyes flatten out and go gray, his mouth parting slightly.

"Yeah?" I ask again.

He shakes his head and smiles at me. "Do you want some OJ?"

"No, I'm fine, thank you."

"It's good for you," he says, pushing the hair that keeps falling over his eyes out of his face.

"No, I'm good, thank you."

He turns around and walks into the wet yard, the sprinklers hissing softly in the distance.

We're lying on the median, I have no idea what street we're on. I'm in La Puente, motherfucking La Puente. I don't even know how to get back home, but I'll get there, sure as shit I'll get there. I touch my cheeks and feel tears spilling from my face. It feels like my eyeballs have sprung a leak. I can't catch my breath and my cheeks hurt.

"Stop, stop," I wheeze.

Mike shakes the can like he's taking a big gulp of air before diving into the ocean. He brings it to his mouth and pushes the nozzle sideways. We snorted K in his room while listening to Portishead, *Dummy*, and ran here. We're on a tear. Or a tear. A page, a drop of saline. He takes a whip and coughs and throws the can, laughing. It hits the road with a clank and I sit up on my elbows and choke out more laughter as I watch it spin and roll into traffic. A car honks, its bright white lights obscuring everything but the steady stream of tires. "Oh shit!" I wheeze. "You can't throw it man, you'll cause a crash."

"Ha!" he shouts. "Give me your can, yo."

I shake the can like I'm about to go deep-sea diving, and spray the inside of the paper bag. Hot pink drips in bloody streams along the inside. Mike paws for it but I pull away. "Me first!" I say, holding it up to my nose and sucking. The bag shrivels like the lung of a dying man. I take another huff and fall back into the grass. I hand the bag to Mike and close my eyes, little fits of giggles petering out between coughs.

"If I could suck off one person I would suck off Chris Isaak," he says, turning and looking at me. He reaches toward my face and touches my lips with his index finger. I take in a huge gasp of air and release the last dirty breath inside me. I feel my cheeks warm and close my eyes. He palms the side of my face and I open again. The blue-green of his irises has been pushed to the edge of nonexistence by his black pupils, expanding and growing larger each day, every hour. The beauty of them, the gorgeousness of them, though. They're still there, quiet and patient on the outside, waiting for the swell to recede so they can return, come home and rest where they belong, in the open; brave and delicate and shining.

All the parts of who I am are alive at his touch. My breath slows and he moves his fingers lightly against my cheek. Grazing the outside of me. "You're beautiful," he says.

"You're the most beautiful person I've ever seen,"

I return. We've always been in love, since the first time we saw each other in Algebra last semester. I'd seen him before, had been watching him since sophomore year and now here we are.

"It doesn't mean anything. It doesn't get me in the house."

I grab his hand and bring it to my mouth. "Michael." He lets me part my lips on his loose fist. "I'm so high," I whisper.

"You'll be okay, you'll come down."

"And what about you?"

"We're the same fucked-up joke."

"Oh yeah?"

"Our ancestors killed and raped our other ancestors."

"Everybody's a thief."

"No. Not everyone. Not us. We were colonized."

"Yes, everyone. Even you."

"I'm a bean burrito and government cheese."

"At least you're the right kind of burrito."

"I don't know what that means," he says. "At least you're not an AIDS burrito."

"You don't have AIDS."

"How do you know?"

"Do you?"

"No. I don't think so, not yet."

I shake my head and smile. He exhales and his breath smells like paint and he has whip cream in the crease of his mouth. I leave it. I imagine kissing him and tasting it. Running my tongue along it.

"I would fuck the shit out of him," he says softly. He pulls me in and we hold each other.

"'Blue Hotel' is the only song."

"Of all the songs, it's the only one," he chokes, starting to cry.

We lie like that and even out into one another, our lungs rising and falling in jerky fits, the red and white head- and taillights passing on either side.

×

"Stop, stop!" yells Mr. Hessler. Everyone stops marching, sweat rolling down our foreheads. I look in the long dance mirrors and lean against the bar, my head resting on my chest. "What is that, Ms. Darling?" My head snaps up and I can feel all eyes turn in my direction. Hell, I can see them; like some bad version of *Suspiria*, the mirrors have turned against me, like I always knew they would.

"What?"

"What do you think?" he asks, resting on his cane. He pounds the wood floor with it. I look outside through the open window behind the piano and into the hills. Below us in the courtyard Cal State LA students scurry to and from their classes. I am continuously amazed at how we walk amongst the newly legal and enlightened. They have an air of bravery unknown to our hunched shoulders, even the ones that probably drive home to do their laundry order their sausage biscuits in the food court with a sense of newly minted entitlement. We must seem so strange to them, brightly colored weirdos clogging up the hallways, loud and boisterous in our fake liberty, oozing teenage rebellion.

My mind is a restless wandering blank. I scan the faces of my fellow thespians and feel dizzy. I am not a friend of a single one. Mr. Hessler walks toward me, his large straw hat flouncing on his head, his open white linen shirt flapping lightly in the breeze that carries through the open window, his gray T-shirt underneath. He is a wrinkled Kleenex. "What are you wearing?" The room has hushed itself to a deathly quiet. I can see out of the corner of my eye as everyone inches back against the mirrors, wiping at their foreheads.

"I think I need water, I don't think I was breathing enough. I feel light-headed."

"That's because you smoke cigarettes before you walk into my classroom, Ms. Darling. You smoke cigarettes before we do Jerzy Grotowski. Before we do Tadashi Suzuki! The unbelievable idiocy of it! Do you understand these methods, the absolute importance of the physicality that they require? I see you outside my office smoking cigarettes. You think just because we are on a college campus you can flaunt your cigarette smoking in our faces? This campus, this freedom, is a privilege. No one is forcing you to be here, Ms. Darling. Do you have any idea how many other students across the city are waiting for an opportunity to get into this school? Ready to jump at the chance to take your place, and you have the gall, the audacity to stand in front of my dance studio and smoke cigarettes?"

"Mr. Hessler, I'm—"

"Shut up!" he yells with usual dramatic flair. He spins around on his cane then hooks it under my tank top strap and yanks. "I asked you a question. *What* are you wearing?"

Everything inside tells me not to but some other part I can't control pushes past me. I try to hold on but it's too late, it slips beyond the person that I want to be and reinforces the person that I am. "Chanel." There's an audible muffled response as the other students cover their mouths trying not to laugh. Mr. Hessler's nostrils flare and he shoves me in the chest with the cane.

"You think this is a joke, young lady? You think this opportunity is a joke?"

"No, sir."

"Let me assure you that attending this school is a privilege and to *shit* on that privilege is to undermine the efforts of the students who get up every day at four a.m. and take the train here, it's to *shit* on the students whose parents couldn't afford to send them to Crossroads but who had the good fortune and talent to get in here. It's to *shit* on everyone that walks into this room having memorized their work, it's to *shit* on your peers that don't come in reeking of marijuana with red eyes, my dear."

"Yes, sir."

"Do I make myself clear?"

"Yes."

"What are you wearing?"

"A tank top."

"Where are your theater clothes?"

"In my locker."

"And why are they in your locker?"

"I, um, I." I look down and my face turns hot. I feel the click in my chest, a roller coaster car grinding and crawling slowly toward the top. It's resting there ready to fall off, the hot burn around my eyes. I hold them back, I clench my fists like I'm sitting in front of the hottest boy at school and holding in a fart.

"You *what*?" he spits in his haughty fake British accent that comes and goes.

I don't know why but I can't find the words to lie and all I can think to do is tell the truth. I just want him to leave me alone. I want everyone to leave me alone. I open my mouth and the car releases, hurtling so many miles an hour down the drop. I wipe my cheeks trying to pretend they aren't wet. I pray that he lets me go but he persists.

"You *what*?" he shouts again.

"I threw up on my shirt."

"You vomited on your shirt? Is that your final answer?"

"Yeah, I barfed." I can hear the students behind me laugh. Fuck, fucking fuck.

"You're not excused, but you're excused from the exercise. You can sit at the piano until class is over and then you and I are going to have a talk, understood?"

"Yes, Mr. Hessler."

"Get water if you need and come back."

"Thank you, thank you so much."

He turns around toward the class and I slink quietly to sit on the old peeling piano bench and hang my head in shame. *Blue hotel, on a lonely highway. Blue hotel, life don't work out my way. Blue hotel, every room is lonely.*

"Everyone resume positions!" The lot of them, the whole sweaty lot raise their right legs in unison. Mr. Hessler slams the cane gesticulating grandly for them to begin marching. They march in a circle, their heads don't bob, their arms out straight at their sides. They reek. They stink.

"Recite!" he yells, and they all freeze, their mouths open, and he slams the cane again. They stomp once then yell together, a great thundering chorus.

×

"I know what you're doing," says Dan, sliding up at my locker. He punches my butt with his fist.

"Ow, you asshole."

"I get it now, I get you. You're just like my fucking mother."

"What are you talking about, dick breath? Get out of my way, I'm meeting someone."

"I know it isn't Chelo cos I had Figure Drawing with her Tuesday and she said you guys haven't kicked it in a minute."

"So what? We had a fight, big deal. It's over, we're good."

"Nuh-uh. I have your number, I finally have it."

"Shut up, stupid," I say, throwing the plastic bag with

my theater clothes into my backpack. "Of course you have my number, I'm your fucking carpool."

"It's an expression, estúpida, and I *was* your carpool, and don't forget this." He shoves his arm into my locker as I slam it shut.

"Your fucking History book bitch! Jesus! You smashed my arm." He looks at me, rubs his elbow. "We have History in the morning."

"Thanks," I say, grabbing the book and heading down the hallway. He chases after me.

"Hey, man, what's your enchilada? Relax, dude." Dan sticks out his injured arm again like I'm crossing the street and a car's about to hit me.

"What, stinko? Can I, like, help you?"

"Yeah. Let's go to my place and get stoned. My mom's at Dr. Green's."

"Clean the ass wax out of your ears. I'm meeting someone." I walk again toward the bright outdoors.

"No, you're not. I saw him get into some dude's car. An old Falcon or something gross pulled up and he got in." I stop and grab my pager. It only reads 4:30. I sigh and look around the hallway, the orange-and-yellow lockers close in like suffocating hands around my throat. "Come on. Let's go to my place. I'll drive, you won't have to take the bus." He takes my arm and starts to pull me and I yank it away.

"Who do you think you are?" I yell. My feet pick me up and I run out into the cool outdoors, into the blinding sun.

"Nicole!" he shouts, but I hurry down the steps toward

F lot. I can hear him behind me but I don't give a fuck. My eyes unhinge from my face and for the second time in two hours I'm sobbing. They're floating orbs bouncing on salty brine, lifting up into the white light that pierces from the inside out. I am distinctly aware that this might be the most dramatic moment of my life thus far. In all my sixteen years on earth I have never been so overwhelmed by my own emotion. How could Mike leave with another man. How could he leave me when we had plans? I step outside and watch myself running. I'm floating on top. Sailing above myself. I push past the dancers in their leotards standing in a circle at the bottom of the stairs.

"Hey, watch it!" shouts Tanya from English. We've exchanged notes before and I knock her off her pirouette. She turns around and sees it's me. "Nikki!" she yells. "You okay?" But I don't stop. They keep dancing. This shit is so dramatic even I pause to look up at the sky, take a giant gulp of air, shake my head, and look back down.

"Swear to god you're like my fucking mother," Dan says, grabbing my arm from behind and pulling me down the parking lot aisle. I'm snotting and dripping and I let him take me.

"You smell bad," I say, wiping at my face.

"Come on. Get in." He shoves me toward his small blue hatchback. I open the door and collapse onto the sticky plastic interior. "Jesus Christ, hold it together." He pops the glove compartment and pulls out a small rolled-up plastic sandwich bag. "You ever taken a Xanax before?" I shake my head. "Swallow this and wipe your face, you'll be okay.

Do you want ice cream?" I shake my head again. "Yes, you do. I do. Let's go to Thrifty. I'll buy."

"I'm not hungry."

"I don't care. I am." He starts the engine and shoves into first gear. He shakes his head, mumbling curses under his breath. "What's your problem? Why are you chasing after him? He's gay, what part of *fucks men* don't you understand?"

"I will jump out of this car if you even try to talk to me about this."

"I'm talking to you as your friend."

"Shut the fuck up you narcissistic asshole. All you want is to know that I want to fuck you. You don't give a shit about me. So what? Fine, yeah, I'd fuck you, you fucking asshole. You don't even want to fuck me anyway so what's the fucking point except to jack off your massive ego?"

"That's a lot of fucks for a virgin."

"*Shut up!*" I scream at the top of my lungs.

"What do you want?" he asks, looking at me. He pops the glove compartment again and grabs the smokes.

"My life is so déjà vu."

"How so?" he asks, grabbing the pack and pushing in the lighter. I wait till it pops. He holds it up and I lean in, inhale, and trace my lip looking out the window. "Tell me."

"Stupid fights in cars, people asking me what I want. What do you want, dick face? Huh? You're sixteen, tell me right now everything you want until you die."

"I'm seventeen. I was held back, remember? And I don't know."

"Exactly. So how come everyone expects me to have an answer?"

"Because you're smart and it's obvious you aren't trying."

"Oh, Jesus Christ, you're my mother too now?"

"Your mom is cool."

"I don't want to barf twice in one day."

"You threw up today?"

"Yeah, while changing for Arts."

"Oh man. For real?"

"Mike and I took the bus to school together. We whipped till three a.m. I didn't sleep. I ate French fries for lunch and barfed."

"Nikki, what the fuck."

"We were supposed to get pancakes after class."

"So what, you're doing speed now?"

"No. *You* do speed and big deal if I am."

"I do coke. Not tweak. I'm not interested in getting ass raped by dirty old men."

"How come you two get to do whatever the fuck you want?"

"Because no one's at home waiting for us."

"Well, see there? Look, you just said it yourself. I get to do speed too, then. No one's at home waiting for me. Sell me an eight ball, I'm wounded."

"Pass the tissues we all have issues. You know what I mean."

"No, you think you know what you mean. You don't get shit, Dan. You think you're some Zen Buddha that can sail through life not hurting people and not getting hurt but you live in such a twisted world of disillusionment. You're seventeen, and I give you ten years before your liver is a spongy piece of shit. Like, like a flag blowing through the wind, a sail or whatever."

"What?"

"I don't know, with holes in it! You're an alcoholic!"

"What do you want from me, man? You want to date me, is that it? You want to fuck me and we can hold hands or something? Chill out, like right now. I mean it. Get that? Chill out, I'm losing my patience."

I don't say anything and look out the window again. Trying to count the helicopters over downtown, far far far in the distance, and the stars I cannot see yet know are there, and the UFOs. *Strange things are afoot at the Circle K.*

"Do you know when the Mongols ruled China?" he asks, turning and smiling at me, reciting our favorite line from *Bill and Ted*.

"How did you know I was just thinking that?"

"Okay, then what number am I thinking of?" he asks, keeping it going.

"Sixty-nine!" I shout, then smile a little, exhale. Maybe he's right. Maybe everything is just okay. "You're clever," I say, looking at him.

"Wanna trash the San Dimas football field with TP?"

"No," I say laughing.

"Wanna break into Raging Waters and look for Napoleon?"

"No!" I say sternly and amused. "You're crazy. We'd get arrested. What would be our defense?"

"Sorry dudes, we were wheezing the juice."

"Eww, no. How dare you mix-quote Encino Tard with Bill and Ted? How could you betray the SGV like that?"

"How could I betray good taste like that. Shit, I'm sorry, that's like comparing elevator music to Bach."

"Yeah, clearly elevator music—"

"Is better!" we shout in unison.

"Do you feel Mexican?"

He shakes his head and laughs softly, pulls a smoke and lights it. "You're so weird. What kind of question is that? You don't?"

"No."

"Well, you shouldn't. You aren't. I mean, not like me and Chelo. You're, you know, American."

"You're American."

"You and Jess are American."

"Jess is Jewish."

"And other stuff. My kids will be like you. I live in the United States but the United States doesn't want me. Look, you live in Pasadena. I live in El Monte. It's not the same."

"*And* you live in South Pasadena."

"Yeah, but that's not my house. That's my mom's boy-friend's house, ya know?"

"You live there. You were born here."

"Yeah and my brother was born in Jalisco. I'm an immigrant. Doesn't matter if I'm not actually. Doesn't matter what you really are. You know that. It's how people see you. What difference does it make if I was born here if my father gets talked down to like a piece of dogshit under someone's shoe and I have to watch it? That's my father."

"You're weirdly wise."

"Duh."

"Your mom though—"

"Is beautiful. She's got that. Now's she's got Dr. Green to pay her bills. Good for her."

"And so what, you're supposed to be like Peter Pan now or whatever?"

"She comes home. She leaves money. I'm not mad."

"I find that hard to believe. When was the last time she came home?"

"A week ago." Dan turns the corner with one hand and reaches into the back seat with his other and grabs his backpack. He unzips it and pulls out a tape. "*My War*," he says, holding up the Black Flag cassette.

I nod and smile, give a thumbs-up. "He's like me."

"Mike? Yeah. He looks like a gringo."

"You're American, too. Mexico is in America."

"Tell that to the gabachos. You know what I mean."

"Yeah. I do. Mike surfs."

"I know. I've seen him. He goes out to Point Dume. He's good. He surfs alone."

"Is that supposed to be some sort of weird metaphor?"

Dan laughs and shakes his head. "You're a real character, kiddo."

"Don't call me kiddo."

"His mother is blond."

"His mother's dead."

"I know that, too."

"They make him sleep in the garage."

"You can't start this shit. God, it's like I'm watching your bad dude habits in their infancy. Don't spend the next twenty years of your life chasing men you can't have. Like, emotionally unavailable dudes."

"How come we've never talked like this before?"

"Like what?"

"I don't know, like grown-ups or whatever."

"Nikki, I'm not an idiot."

"Then why do you act like a Neanderthal?"

"Fuck you, man."

"Whatever."

"And what makes you so mature? You're about as mature as a toddler. You just had a tantrum and ran out of school. Who gives a shit. You high yet?"

"I don't know. I feel calmer."

"Yeah, you're high. So what, you're a fag hag now? Nikki, he is a gay young man. That means he fancies the company of other men. Anyway, there are plenty of guys in school who would do you."

"Geez god, how many times do I have to tell you?"

"Ugh, fine. I know. There are plenty of guys at school who would enjoy your company." We stop at a red light and he looks at me. "Who *do* enjoy your company."

"What? Quit being weird." He shakes his head and we drive down Main toward the Thrifty off Atlantic. He swims close but never docks the boat and I'm never ever

ever filling in the blanks for him again only to be mocked. He only wants a warm dick hug anyway. I watch an old Asian couple push their cart filled with long beans and wrapped fish from the Pan Asian market around the corner. They are hunched over, her wearing a floppy straw hat and him a Dodgers baseball cap and blue Sta-Prest pants. A kid on a skateboard swerves around them and yells something in Cantonese or perhaps Mandarin that sounds like *Get out of the way*. His head has been shaved to stubble except for a loose, shiny ponytail that rests on top of his head and two long sections of hair that hang above his temples and frame the sides of his face. The old couple stops. He jumps off his skateboard wiping sweat from his forehead with his oversized white T-shirt and exposes rippled and tattooed stomach muscles, a pager clipped to his khaki Dickies.

"Asian bangers man," Dan whispers, "are so hard. I bet he has a gat. Or at least a rice rocket." I roll my eyes. We sit at the stoplight and watch him. He's waiting with us so he can cross.

"How am I like your mom?"

"I bet he has a Honda with one of those souped-up engines. I love those things. Fuck yeah! I know I'm supposed to be, like, into lowriders or whatever cos I'm brown, but fuck, I'm into speed. You know? *Zmmm, zmmm!*" he mouths, making little engine sounds and fake turning a wheel. "It's like a skateboard you can ride inside of."

"If he had a car he wouldn't be on a skateboard. How am I like your mom?"

"You don't know that, smarty-farty pants. I ride my board all over town."

"How am I like your mom?"

"You keep thinking some dude is going to solve all your problems. Her I get, you I don't get it. You're a teenager, man. Have a little confidence, you're a cute girl."

"I guess thanks."

"You're beautiful, Nikki," he says matter-of-factly, turning the corner, and I can feel myself blush. I look at him, weird and hot. His stupid fucking face.

×

I walk in and Mom is in the bedroom stuffing clothes in a suitcase and crying.

"What's wrong?" I ask, setting my backpack down beside the door. She spins around, her face a wild mess of rage.

"What's wrong with you?" she cries, throwing a shoe at me. I duck and it misses. "I wish I could hit you. God, I wish I could just knock you out."

"Mom—"

"Where the fuck have you been, you little idiot? Two days? You go missing for *two fucking* days?" She strangles a pair of rolled-up socks and shakes them at me, her fist bulging. "You little *shit*! I told you to return a movie! A fucking movie!"

"Mom, I'm sorry."

"You made me call your father! Your goddamn father!

Go in your room, I don't want to look at you. I'm coming home Tuesday."

"Where are you going?"

"Oh, well, my dear," she says, standing up and pushing a handful of hair over her forehead. She puts her hands on her hips and glares at me. "Let me tell you, you picked a real lousy time to teach me a lesson, let me tell you that. Your sister called. I have to go."

"Wait, all the way to San Francisco? What happened?"

"Santa Cruz. She's in some motel out there. I don't know, some goddamn shit with that *boy*. I have to go see her, that's all."

"Is she okay? Is she coming back with you?"

"I don't know, maybe. Clean your grandpa's old room and get it nice while I'm gone, huh? Just in case?"

"Sure."

"Can I trust you?"

"Yes, of course."

"I put two hundred dollars in the jewelry box. That should cover your food and gas till I get back."

"Okay. You're leaving the car?"

"Yes, I called a cab, I'm headed to Bob Hope. Honey, I'm sorry. You deserve more than this, I'm sorry."

"Mom, it's cool."

She reaches out and grabs my chin and tugs on it. I flinch. "My big girl."

I back away and her hand falls. She looks down then back at me, her eyes low.

"Mija, you take a lot. I'm proud of you, all right?"

"I know, Mom. If Lyla's hurt, go."

"Okay," she says, zipping up the bag and walking toward the living room. She opens the front door covered in shadows. "I love you, honey."

I wonder if she's aware of what she says to me, if she ever remembers anything at all. Maybe I have two mothers and they fight each other like Regan and Pazuzu dueling it out and it's always a mystery who might win.

×

Chelo slides up to me in the hallway.

"You baked?" I ask.

"Naw, I wish. You got any?"

"No but I can grab Dan."

"Oh yeah, grab Dan," she says smiling.

"And Jess?"

"Ugh, no. I mean, Jess is cool but I can't handle her rich-girl shit right now. It's my moon time. Don't feel like dealing with her, *like fer sure*, ya know?"

"Come on," I say, cocking my head. "I bet she'll drive and take us to eat." I bring my hands to my chest and bat my eyelashes.

"No, man, you *come on*. You only like her cos you're white."

"You're majorly spaced out, man."

"Puta, don't start with me, I mean it, I'll pow pow you."

"Fine, chale, estúpida." I slam my locker and we head out toward the courtyard. She's wearing a short army skirt like Tank Girl, a vintage seventies *Star Wars* shirt with an authentic press-on Darth Vader, and has shaved her eyebrows and drawn them back on with sharpie. Her hair is candy-apple red and hangs long and parted down the middle like a hippie. Her combat boots lace all the way up her thigh. "Dude, you look sexy," I say, glancing at her ensemble.

"My ensamblay impresses you?" she says, imitating my voice, again.

"Like, oh my gawd! It totally does! Like, it's so spicy!" I say, imitating her imitating me. We make our way to F lot talking like spaced-out eighties chicks.

"Like, what do you think his dick looks like?"

"Oh my gawd, like I totally bought a tubular blouse at the Galleria! I wonder if it will match his wiener?"

"Have a 'tude, wiener cock dude!"

Jessica comes running out of music hall waving her arms and heading in our direction.

"Oh my god, dudes," she says, leaning on her side and trying to catch her breath. "I am so baked, I need to scarf. Carrows, South Pas? My treat? I totally need to inhale some chipotle chicken fingers, like, stat."

Chelo and I burst into guffaws and Jess's face gets all twisted and embarrassed and she looks down at herself trying to figure out what we're laughing at.

"How's Encino?" asks Chelo, trying to control her laughter.

"I live in Sherman Oaks," she answers, not understanding she's being made fun of, because who would ever make fun of her? "Come on, dudes, are we going to eat or what?" she whines, tugging on the bottom of her shirt. "I am, like, totally famished and stuff."

"You're baked?" asks Chelo.

"Totally. Wanna blaze?"

"For totes," she quips, looping her arm in Jessica's like they're Laverne and Shirley and I can't tell if she's faking it or not.

"Ándale, stupids!" she yells, turning her head in my direction. "Órale! I got some pancakes to scarf!" And she gives me an exaggerated wink. Jessica wraps her arms around Chelo and they hug and kiss each other's cheeks, and they aren't faking it anymore, it's good times. Jess leans all her weight on Chelo and keeps trying to not fall over and their lunch boxes drag along the floor.

"Stop it, loony toon!" yells Chelo, shoving Jess. "Come on slow poke!" she calls looking at me again where I'm trailing behind. Her face is bright and light and laughter leads our way.

"Okay!" I call, picking up my feet and jogging after them. "I'm coming!"

×

Chelo's parents are at the wooden kitchen table, their backs to us. We walk in and her mom turns around, her front bangs a rolled-up swoop like my grandma's in old photographs. She cocks her head back, eyebrows thin, her seventies plaid shirt tucked into denim bell-bottoms, her lips lined in thick brown eyeliner, her face packed in thick foundation, her lips a deep scarlet red. "Where you been at?" she says, pulling buds off a dried marijuana batch and stacking them on top of an even larger pile of naked stems. Chelo's father, Dodgers shirt tucked into beige Dickies and wearing brown chanclas and white tube socks, stands and starts to push the weed into a large Vons paper bag rolled down at the top.

"Let's go in the back," he says to Chelo's mom. "You all make some food, hang out. Chelly, you need money for food?"

"Yeah," she says putting her hands on her hips. "You don't have to go in the back." She raises her eyebrows at him.

"You wish, little fish. We're going in the back."

"Don't be getting no ideas, estúpida," adds her mom, absentmindedly picking dirt from underneath her long lacquered red nails, glossier and shinier than any hot rod. My eyes wander to the counter and I see a small black handgun. My heart flutters and I avert my eyes.

"Ah shit, mija," says her dad watching me. He grabs a large T-shirt off the kitchen table and walks over to the counter and snatches it, walks it to the fridge and places it delicately, still shrouded, on top. "I'm sorry, shit, I'm sorry. Look, mija," he takes his wallet out, hands Chelo twenty dollars, "Go get some food, anything. Get a video too," he says, handing over the Blockbuster card.

Chelo's mom walks up to him and grabs the money. "Fuck, sit, I'll make you guys dinner. What do you want?"

she asks, tying an apron around her waist. "I can make cheeseburgers or fideo, how 'bout that?"

"That sounds really good, actually," I say, looking at Chelo, who pulls a chair and sits.

"We just had chicken fingers, fool," she says, looking at me.

"Mary, them kids don't need you to cook, they good with chips and snacks, they just ate, they wanna hang out."

"No, it's cool," says Chelo, looking at her mother's face, which deflates softly at her father's words. "Actually that does sound good. Thanks, Mom, I want a cheese-burger."

"Mija, I love you," she says, grabbing Chelo's mouth and squeezing. She walks to the fridge, pulls out pre-shaped hamburger patties, a block of cheddar cheese, a jar of pickles, and a container of tomato paste. She grabs a can of RO*TEL from the cupboard, a container of garlic salt, and red chili powder. "Get the hamburger buns from the pantry." Chelo and I stand and walk toward the back-door. On the couch is a small child, five years old, eating a Lucas chili candy pop and holding a can of Coke.

"Where's your mom at?" asks Chelo, stopping to look at the kid, her niece. "Hey, Flora, estúpida," she says, tapping the girl on the side of her head, "where's your puta mom at?"

"Don't call your sister fucking nasty names in front of her daughter!" yells her mom from the kitchen where she's smashing the preformed hamburger patties into a large bowl with all the other ingredients, giving them new shapes.

"Adelicia!" screams Chelo. "Your baby fell on its face! Get down here!"

"Who are you?" demands her mom, walking toward us, hamburger meat on her hands. "What kind of nonsense are you *even* stirring? Shut up and get those patty buns."

"Adelicia!" she screams again.

"What, puta?" screams Adel from upstairs.

"Your baby's ugly!"

"Fuck you, stupid!" she shouts, flipping her long straight hair over her shoulder and walking back around the corner toward her room and slamming the door.

"Momma, can we grab a joint?"

"What?" she says, screwing up her face. She drops her hands in the bowl and looks at us like we're strangers that walked into her house and started shouting demands. And then I realize that right now, to Mary, we are. Who are we? Who are we really except dumb stoned teenagers fucking up her rhythm?

"I know you're joking. Shit," she says, rolling her eyes and massaging the patties.

"Whatever, I'll just grab one later."

"Nuh-uh, oh hell no!" yells her mom, walking into the living room ready to scream at Chelo, but we've already opened the side door to the pantry and are beyond her reach. The door swishes closed on her pissed-off face.

"I got 'em!" yells Chelo, pulling the hamburger bun

bag toward her. "It's okay, Mommy, I got it. Got the buns! Come on," she says, tossing them on the washing machine and walking into the backyard instead of going back into the kitchen. Her father sits on a cinder block in the yellowed sea of weeds and old cars, engines missing and spilling guts into the dried earth. The hot yellow sun sets on the low flat city of Montebello. "Daddy, can we have a joint?" He shakes his head and laughs like she's Wally Cleaver and just got caught sticking her finger in a pie. Incorrigible.

"Yeah, yeah, okay, come on."

I try to navigate my way around the broken parts of the yard toward where he's sitting with the money and the weed. Chelo struggles too, stepping on old tires and trying to avoid the sharp burs and stickers that reach up from the ground like claws.

It's not easy, but we make it, and he's there with open arms, a big toothy smile on his face, the sun arching ever so beautifully like a ball of fire, a golden ring. "Mija, mija," he says, pulling her into him, her feet lifting off the ground. "Come, come."

×

What if I set the house on fire? What if I turn into a bird and fly away, turquoise, purple, like the world of Sandra Cisneros and her Mango Streets? What if I stack these novels up in a corner and shoot them down like beer cans in a field? Sitting on the stumps of fir trees in the backwoods of New Mexico? What if I become a badger in Walden Pond? What if I watch Henry each morning gather water for his coffee? What if I stick my head in this speaker on a Wednesday night in the giant trashed-out banquet hall, former grand beauty of the Alexandria Hotel, downtown? Happy hardcore blasting my eardrums into outer space, kids dressed as anime characters doing bumps of K out of PEZ dispensers with Scooby-Doo heads? What if I tell you instead that I like to get fucked up? What if I tell you I like to hit my head on walls as hard as I can because the dizzy feeling is the most delicious thing I've found after fucking cucumbers in my room at night, staring at pictures of Marlon Brando I've ripped out of library books? What if I tell you I *like* to fall down? What if I told you that when I get stoned I spin in a circle till my legs drop out beneath me then beat my temples against my fist then stand again, to try and see how far I can walk? What if I told you about getting high? Would you believe me if I told you I get high all day? Even if you can't see me, even if you try to talk to me, even if you ask me to stand at the chalkboard and read from my final, even if you ask me to stay after class, I have another eyelid, it's invisible, it's a film, and you'll never see it, and it's just enough to keep me shrouded and floating from this world to the next.

Let me tiptoe around you on the highway of life. Every cigarette is a firecracker. Let me explode on my own.

Jessie calls and asks if I want to spend the weekend at her place. "I can take you to school Monday no probs."

"Yeah, that would be cool, actually. My mom is gone till tomorrow."

"Where is she?"

"I don't know. She just left," I lie, because I don't want to get into the Lyla thing and also I just don't care. Jessica interprets this, however, as my needing her charity. My poor unfortunate soul.

"Well, fuck, are you okay? Hold on. Mom!" she screams.

"Jessie, Jessica, it's cool, it's not one of those situations."

"*Situations?* Well, fuck, Nikki, I never thought that you were like, that you needed . . ."

"Like what? Need what?" I ask, sitting up straight, my interest piqued. "Like what?" I ask again, trying not to sound defensive or challenging. I must remain, even in this moment, racially ambiguous. *Say it.* I can hear Sparks's "I Predict" playing in her bedroom.

"Nothing, I just, where's your mom?"

"Up north."

"Up north where? Why?"

"Half Moon Bay. Everything is fine. She had a work thing."

"Oh. Okay. Are you sure?"

"Yeah dude, I'm sure."

"You live in Pasadena? I'll come get you right now."

"It's cool."

"You . . . do live in Pasadena, right?"

"Yeah, man, a nice little white neighborhood."

"That's not what I meant."

"Sure it is."

"You know what, man? I'm sick of being accused of being racist. You guys don't even know me. I'm Jewish, how can I be racist? Why are you guys always even *talking* about race? I mean, come on, *who cares?*"

"I don't think you're racist, Jess," I say calmly, turning one of my emerald-green pieces of costume jewelry over in my hand. I hold it up to my neck in front of the mirror. And I don't think she's racist. "I think you're classist."

"What is your deal, weirdo?"

I hang up and let the dial tone wipe my brain clean. Yes. Yes. Clean me through.

I walk down the street to Sarah's house smoking a cigarette, even though I know my neighbors can probably see me. Climb the brick wall that separates her street from mine and hop down into the backyard. Her lawn is green and overgrown and their trampoline, the one we jumped on as kids until our heads almost exploded, sits covered in red, yellow, and brown rotting autumn leaves. The ground is wet and I get mud on my combats. "Hey," I say, leaning against the screen door to her family's basement. "Fuck!" she shouts, jumping up and knocking a bowl of cereal off her lap. Luckily it's dry. She's watching *Animaniacs, Pinky and the Brain,* and I know that she's probably been sitting here since eight a.m. drooling at Saturday morning cartoons. "You scared me," she says. I pull the screen door open and walk inside. The Lefkowitzs have lived in the same house since 1974 and that was the last time they decorated. The brown shag carpet is matted like an old sheepdog and the basement, with her older brother Marc's drums and old Rush and Led Zeppelin posters, makes it feel as if you're stepping into a time machine. Only Sarah's old Cabbage Patch Kids, My Little Ponies, and dirty Rainbow Brite, which she brought downstairs in junior high, offer some evidence of the progression of time. Any signs of the current decade, like Chris Cornell or Kathleen Hanna, remain upstairs, thumbtacked to her bedroom wall.

"It smells like schwag down here," I say, sniffing the air and helping her pick up Honey Smacks.

"That's because I got baked like an hour ago."

"Where's your mom?" I ask, sitting next to her on the couch once the cereal has been collected and put back into its bowl.

"Upstairs."

"Well, are you doing anything today?"

"Like what?" she asks, looking back at the TV. Brain presses his hands together, an evil mastermind and shoots Pinky with a zap of red light.

"Gee, I don't know, something?" I pick up her pager. "How are you going to get a life if you never turn this thing on?"

"I have a life," she says, eating the cereal from the bowl. "I fucked Paul Kinsey last night. What did you do?"

Paul Kinsey is a freshman at Occidental that she met at the Norton Simon Museum and now picks her up from school sometimes. He is, admittedly, hot.

"Ew. That guy's a scab."

Finally she looks at me, annoyed. "What is your problem, man? It's like, eleven a.m."

I put the pager down. "Nothing, I just, I want to get out of here."

"Okay, like where?" she looks at my Siouxsie and the Banshees shirt. "Nice outfit. Your dream of becoming the next Exene Cervenka is almost complete. Is it real?" she pulls on the hem, which is ripped.

"Yeah, got it at the Salvation Army store on Melrose, the boots too."

"What about the pants?" she asks, looking at the black skintight jeans.

"Aaardvarks."

"The eyeliner's cool."

"Thanks," I say. "Hey! Let's hike to the top of Echo Canyon and creep the abandoned hotel."

"I don't know," she says, watching Pinky. "That seems like a lot of work."

"Well I don't want to spend all day in your basement getting stoned."

"No one asked you to come over."

"Don't make me leave."

"No one's making you do anything."

"Let's go to the Banana Museum!"

"That place smells. I'll go to Old Town."

"It's full of babies."

"No it's not."

"Yes, it is. It's just a bunch of junior high kids. What about Poo-Bah's?"

Finally she looks at me and smiles. "Okay, that place is solid. Let me take a shower and change. Cash the pipe." She jogs up the brown carpeted steps toward the upper part of the house, her long, shiny black hair bouncing as she goes, and I can't help but notice that I like her navy blue flared corduroy pants with the sailor front. I lean forward and grab the sandwich bag of weed and load the one hitter. "You had sex last night?" I shout, looking for a lighter on the dirty coffee table. She pokes her head back downstairs and gives me a dirty look. "Shut up, man," she says, shushing me. "My mom is, like, somewhere."

Poo-Bah's, the old record store run by a couple of burned-out, long-white-haired hippies with yellow mustaches from years of nicotine and weed smoke, sits inside a dusty old bungalow in Pasadena and houses one of the finest collections in all of Los Angeles County. Half of it stapled to the old house's walls. Every inch covered with masterworks from Jim Morrison to Os Mutantes to the Police, Black Flag, Harry Belafonte, and Keely Shaye Smith. The ceiling is covered as well, a virtual time capsule of the last thirty years of hepcats and rockers, autographed head shots looking down on you like the smiling heads of gods. *Hey, Grand Poo Bah, a real Honey! Love, Dolly P! Never close your doors, mate, Keef Richards.*

Sarah's currently got half the store under her arm. I flip through the punk section looking for a Weirdos album

Chelo told me about. I pretended like I knew who they were and now I'm under self-imposed pressure to catch up on my lie before I see her next. I can't find it and Sarah walks up to the old wooden register, the front counter-top piled high with rock books, moldy *LA Weekly*s, chattering wind-up teeth, and a plastic chicken that hangs to the side of the counter, stapled by its feet. She opens her mouth to announce her presence, one foot on the small stool put in place so customers can step up and hand their purchases to one of the old hippies who sit hidden somewhere behind the piles of junk.

"Do you have the Weirdos?" I shout over the stack before she speaks.

"Hey! I was next!" she says, shoving me out of the way. *Dog and Butterfly* by Heart slips from beneath her arm and she kneels down to readjust her pile.

"We're the only ones in here, jerk," I tell her. A white head, an old snowy peak, emerges from behind the pile.

"Sold one last week. Want me to order it?"

"No, it's okay, I'll go to the Tower. What about Team Dresch?"

"Who?" asks Sarah, standing.

"It's queercore," I say.

"We sure do." He emerges from behind the register like the Wizard of Oz, shorter and more human than one would expect. I follow him to the used section and he pulls it out from behind the *T* card. "We've got *Personal Best*, want it?"

"Yes, please," I say nodding. He walks back to the register and climbs the little steps back to his stool. He punches it in and I can hear him place it in a plastic bag. Sarah stands, trying to keep all her records in her grasp, mouth open, like I've just fucked a horse in front of her.

"Rude, much?" she asks, still glaring at me.

"That'll be eight fifty," he says. I hand the money over and he hands the bag down.

"Thanks!"

"Yup," he answers unenthusiastically.

Sarah hands over her records next, head still twisted in my direction in disbelief and disgust.

"Close it," I say, tapping her chin. "You'll catch the airborne herps."

"Oh, this is one of my favorites!" says the disembodied voice of old register hippie. "*American Beauty* was the album that defined the Dead! I listened to this on my drive from New York to LA in '71. Just a record player plugged into a generator in the backseat, bumping along as we went . . ." The old man fades into the background and I can hear Sarah saying some boring business back as she hands more records over. I pull the Dresch album from the bag and look at Donna Dresch's face. It feels cool, real good and cool.

We sit in Garfield Park in South Pasadena, eating sushi we five fingered from Bristol Farms. Sarah starts to pull her albums out and spreads them in front of her, arranged like a fan. She opens *Goats Head Soup*. "I can't wait to listen to this."

"My dad's got that," I say. "It's good, I guess." She puts it back in its sleeve.

"Hey, what's going on between you and Dan? Is this all for him? This punk stuff?"

"What?" I ask, honestly confused. "Dan Martínez?"

"Well, yeah, obviously he likes you."

"Obviously you're crazy. He's nice, I don't know, we have English together. He was my carpool."

"Thanks, by the way, for offering to take me to school."

"Come on, you have Marc's car. I thought you wanted to drive yourself. You made a big deal about it last year."

"Yeah but, he's called you on the phone, right?" she asks, ignoring me.

"He called me once, to invite me to the Malahini."

"You went to the Malahini? You never told me that."

"Yeah I did."

"No you didn't. When?"

"I don't know, like a month ago."

"Well, do you like him?"

I look at Sarah as she bites into a piece of California roll and for a minute, with the sun shining down through the oak trees across her freckles and pale skin, lighting up the green and blue flecks in her eyes and long straight black hair, over her ruffled, hippie button-up shirt with the strawberries and snails on it, and her blue corduroy sailor pants, I see what boys see. Beauty. Her small thin waist and big boobs, pure hot, high school beauty. "I wonder why you aren't more popular."

"What?" she coughs. "What is going on with you, man? Is your brain scrambled in the frying pan or what?"

"It's just that you're so hot, and I'm, like, your only friend."

"Man," she says, putting the container lid on her sushi and stuffing her albums back into their plastic bag. Soy sauce and wasabi drip onto her California rolls. "I want to go home," she says, standing.

"Why?"

"Why? *Why?* Are you crazy? Look, I don't know if I want to hang out for a while. I think you need to, like, reevaluate yourself or whatever."

×

I have the quiet of my imagination. I have the peace of mind given to me by solitude. In Northern California as a child the river ran along the side of my window, yellow, purple, red, green, blue. Rainbow fish leapt above the bank, catching a butterfly caught in the beauty of the sun. I had books. I had me. Myself. I. Later I had music. I have alone, everything this mind can imagine. And here, now, I have you, following me to the end.

×

Lyla lies across the couch, her feet dangling over the edge. Lyla leaves a pair of white dance gloves on the kitchen table, their wrists stained with cover-up. Lyla comes home with a group of kids costumed up like cross-dressing Nazis and heads into her room and slams the door. Cocteau Twins blares out from underneath, making the walls shake. Lyla leaves me locked in the car while she heads across the long parking lot toward the mall, says, don't move. Lyla comes home late and dad comes racing out of the bedroom, fists clenched, shouting. Lyla jumps and covers her face. We're at a Round Table in Gilroy, a little girl across from us in the dark parking lot is pulled from inside the dimly lit restaurant by a father, he's drunk and snarling, she whines and sobs, he's drunk. She knows it but there's nothing she can do, because she's a child and it's time to go home.

×

Chelo and I walk into the party and I can tell things are about to get real cinema tonight. It's a night when this city we live in really shows itself. There is a giant midcentury modern glass wall that hangs over a cliff of the South Pasadena hills and stares straight into Highland Park, Montecito Heights, Lincoln Heights, and downtown. We all sort of pause and bump into one another's heels when we enter the giant wooden 1940s carved oak door. A large bull head resembling Picasso's bull masks is carved into the wood, a gothic bronzed door handle pushing into a prefab castle, and we stare, briefly, dumbfounded. Lights. Buildings. Emerald erect. Emerald contained. Look at it, no wonder we're all fucked up and broken. No wonder we're all high and lazy. No wonder we're all bored and trying to grab on to apathy with every ounce of energy we can muster, every fiber of our souls. No wonder we drink music like water, no wonder we watch movies like food. We are trapped like flies in this bell jar of yuck. We are specimens in God's big joke. A super city of noncity. A city of death and reinvention, glittering arrows of black, pulsating like rockets through the night, ready to pierce the deepest part of our being. Fuck, we're LA kids. We are the kids of LA.

They write books about us. They make after-school specials about us. And none of it is the real us. None of it really captures who we are. But we eat it, digest it, and let it redefine us until we no longer know what is real and what is fake, and how clichéd is that? We are the sticky center of the cliché. We jump off cliffs, Robotrip, slice our wrists, star in TV specials about the sixties, we OD in gutters and slam doors while peeling out of driveways in new and old cars. Sixteen and seething. We fall into swimming pools and float to the bottom. We stand on dark street corners waiting to kill our own, we drive by in cars ready to annihilate our faith in ourselves, ready to destroy that which is most sacred. We bleed. We walk down sidewalks daring the world to photograph us, daring the goddamn place to care. We party, we converge, we weep, we grow weary. Ivy tangled, one hand grabbing the next. A fantasy to behold. A fantasy to be beholden. We live here. We build this shit up and let it break us down. We dissolve into myth. We let authors steal our stories and toss them high into the hills where we spread like wildfire. The smoke of our lives hovers over everything until we have crept into every home, every school, every office and reminded you that this is a city of slash and burn. This is a city ablaze.

Mike yanks on my arm and pulls me toward him. Chelo is in the bright aquamarine pool, her red hair fanning out as she pushes toward the bottom. Small twinkle lights strung through oak trees cover everything in a fairy tale hue of steam and spiraling pools of iridescence. The fluorescent soft yellow pool light creates black shadows of our bodies, moving and talking, laughing and drinking, eating and smoking. We're the oldest kids you know, we're all about a hundred years old.

Chelo is all, *prehistoric*, and then Dan grabs my arm and Mike yanks my arm and the entire place stops and we rise like zombies to the boomtown. *Too much fighting on the dance floor!* Wet, dripping, we look like "Thriller" extras. "Skank, bitches!" shouts Jessica and someone pushes her into the pool. A rainbow roll flies off a tray and over the side of a cliff. Wasabi is, like, all *over* the place. Mike and Dan cannonball, they kick, steam rising around them when they shoot back up, wet serpents, crawling onto land.

We're so cinema. We're so, like, we *own* this, we're so, like, *don't even try*. This? This is *ours*.

×

The lights blossom like midnight flowers, morning glories hang like sleeping bats.

The streets are windy and we wobble.

×

Ms. Lavoi calls my name on the way out of class. My heart sinks and I hang back near the door as other students file out.

"Oh shit, kid," says Dan as he slips into the hallway. I roll my eyes, sit back down, and wait until she shuts the door. We're alone. I swallow.

"It was nice of you to join us this week."

"Yeah, well."

"Listen, you can relax, you're not in trouble, I mean, not with me, at the moment."

"You're excusing my absences?"

"No, I just want to have a conversation." I look down at the floor and start to count the square, flecked 1960s tiles that cover the ground.

"Did you get help on your essay?"

"The Woolf one?"

"Yes."

"No. I wrote it."

She reaches for something on her desk, my paper, and walks to the desk next to mine, sits. "Here." She hands it over. "Look at it."

"You gave me a C," I say, pulling back the first page. "Is that, what? I'm confused, is that considered good now?"

"I gave you a C because it's obvious you wrote this the night before class and because the grammar is atrocious, but I wanted to ask you about the content of the paper. Are these your own ideas or did you read them in a book?"

"No, I mean, yeah, I mean."

"No, yeah, what?"

"They're my own ideas."

"You think Virginia Woolf embraced a masculine projection?"

"Yes."

"The word *projection*. It's not in the foreword or anywhere in the edition I assigned. That was your word choice?"

"Yeah. I mean, I have a brain."

"I know that. Is that a word you use in theater?"

"Yeah. Sometimes. We're reading Dos Passos."

"How is it that they can get you to read Dos Passos, but I ask you to read Virginia Woolf and it's pulling teeth?"

"I didn't actually read the Passos, if it makes you feel better."

"You just said that you did."

"No, I skimmed it."

"And you gleaned the word *projection*? From skimming? What is a projection to you?"

"It's uh, what I said here, in the paper."

"Tell me, use your own words, pretend I haven't read the paper."

"This is weird," I say, getting nervous.

"Nicole, did you write this paper?"

"Yes, of course I did."

"What is a projection to you?"

"God, I dunno, it's like when you pretend to be one

thing in order to either get something you want or to not get bothered trying to do something else. You know, like Vito Andolini in *Godfather II*. He was always coming back for revenge but had to play dumb to get to America. If you want to be left alone you might project being stupid when you're not so people let you coast, I guess." I look down. Green, blue, gold flecks.

"You're not a bad actress."

"Ms. Lavoi, for real this feels exploity."

"Is that the answer you think will convince me to leave you alone?"

"No, that's the answer I believe."

"What's your homelife like?" This is sudden and catches me off guard. "You're very quiet."

"Just in here."

"You don't like English?"

"No, I love English."

"Really?"

"Yeah. Why would I lie about that?"

"I don't know. I don't know very much about you. You read the books I assign, don't you?"

"Of course."

"I know you do. Why read the books and not do the papers?"

"I did this paper."

"Yes, well. If you need to talk to someone, sometime, you can always talk to me."

"How old are you Ms. Lavoi?"

"Thirty-six."

"Are you happy?"

"Sometimes."

"Do you think Virginia Woolf was happy?"

"It would seem not. Have you heard of Sylvia Plath?"

"Sure. She's a poet."

"That's right. She also committed suicide."

"Oh man," I say, even though I already know this, but it seems like Ms. Lavoi gets off on dumping knowledge, and who knows, maybe she took this job to feel like she could make a diff.

"She pioneered something called confessional poetry, I wrote my dissertation on it. Her and another poet, Anne Sexton. She also wrote one novel called *The Bell Jar*."

"Sexton?"

"Plath."

"Sure. Yeah, I know that one. The gothy girls dig it."

"Well, I think you might dig it too, if you gave it a chance. I could lend it to you."

"No, that's okay, I can get it at the library."

"Will you?"

"Sure," I say with a shrug. "I mean, if it's good."

"It is."

"Then, yeah, why not."

"When you're done we can talk about it, yes?"

"Sure, whatever you want."

"It's not what I want that I'm getting at."

"What are you getting at?"

"You're very smart."

"Thank you. Can I go?"

"Okay," she says, standing and walking to her desk. She pulls out a pack of gum from her purse and raises her right eyebrow at me. "You can go."

"Oh, okay," I say, standing. "I'll catch you later."

She smiles and raises her eyebrows once more. Standing in her black jeans, penny loafers, silk button-up, and navy blue men's blazer, I'm hit with a sudden realization, oh shit, Ms. Lavoi is cool.

×

I'm walking down the middle of campus toward the library when I feel someone tug on my backpack strap. I stop and turn around, annoyed.

"Oh, hi," I say, pulling my arms close and leaning on one foot. I grab a piece of hair and stick it in my mouth.

"Hey," says Mike, coughing. He looks at the ground then pushes his hair back and smiles. Warm like sun on your back in a field of shadows. "I'm really sorry about Monday. I forgot George was picking me up."

"It's cool. I got a ride home with Meanstreetz."

"Oh yeah?" he asks, starting to walk. I walk with him. "You like that guy?"

"Eww, no. He's my friend, he's sort of gross."

Mike laughs and nods. "Yeah, I guess." We're silent a while then he stops and I turn and look at him. "You wanna get out of here?"

"I can't. I'm on probation."

"Oh yeah?"

"Yeah."

"Hey, he has sex with lots of girls. Maybe he'd have sex with you."

"Dan? Eww. I don't want to have sex with him."

"Why not?"

"Why does everyone think I want to have sex?"

"No, I meant, he's—"

"He's what?"

"Never mind, I just meant, I don't know, forget it. You wanna get faded? I've got bud."

"Sure, of course."

"Okay, cool. You know, you're prettier than you think you are. You're really pretty."

"Thank you."

"He'd definitely fuck you if you tried."

My heart is perforated and sopping. "No, I mean, if I wanted to I'm sure I could make it happen, but I don't want to."

"Oh hey, I'm done with your painting."

"Really?" I ask, brightening.

"Sure!" he says, also blushing with a smile.

We chuckle a little and keep walking toward the science building on the other side of campus. The roof of which is always empty and prime territory. The Republic of Smokey.

×

We're on the roof, proper baked, lying on our backs. I can hear the bell ring and sit up. I stand and walk to the edge of the cement wall that lines the perimeter and look

115

out over campus. The doors to King Hall shove open and kids flood the steps and head toward F lot. I walk back to where Mike is and lie down again.

"Point one hour till Arts," I say.

"Yeah, I got ears," he snarls, surprising me. It's so un-riddle-like, so clear and sense making.

"Oh, yeah, I mean, of course," I say casually.

"I mean, totally," he says kindly, correcting himself.

For the first time in our brief friendship I wonder if he fakes his interactions with me, if actually he's much sharper than he lets on. "Oh hey, look." He sits up and pulls a folded crinkled piece of paper from his pocket, opens the page carefully. It's a black-and-white picture of Elvis covered in kisses and wearing a lei. It's been ripped from a book.

"You do that, too?" I ask.

"Do what?" he asks defensively, as if I've accused him of something.

"Tear pictures from library books."

"Oh, no," he says, after a long pause. "I found it in the hall."

"Oh cool. He looks cool."

"He is cool."

"I mean, yeah. Duh."

"He's dead."

"No, I mean, of course." Swimming through the mud of our conversation I grab large stones and shove them in my pocket, walking deeper, where I hope to drown. *Shakespeare's sister will put on the body which she has so often laid down.* "I like to write," I say suddenly, surprising myself.

"What?" he asks, confused.

"I don't know, it just came out," I say, laughing. "I mean, I like to read."

"Library books? Is that why you tear pictures out of them?"

"No, I do that because I make collages with the pictures. I like to frame them sometimes. The collages I mean."

He nods. Taking in this useless fact as if it's useful. "What do you like to read?" He sounds kind, distracted. It's like we've never met and were meeting here now at the Republic of Smokey for the first time.

"I'm not sure."

"What did you read last?"

"*Spin*," I answer, honestly.

"Oh," he says, sounding disappointed, "I like to read, too."

But I maintain that she would come if we worked for her, and that so to work, even in poverty and obscurity, is worthwhile.

×

I decide to stay in and listen to CDs. It's nine thirty and the front door opens. I sit up. It's Mom. I can hear her sigh and take off her shoes. She drops the keys in the bowl next to the door. I walk into the living room. She sees me and gives a weak smile. She seems tired. I walk to her and bury my head in her chest and she wraps her arms around me. "Mommy," I say. She pulls me close and I breathe in the pine needle scent. She has sap on her flower apron and it smells good.

"Did you eat?" she asks walking toward the kitchen, her arm still around me. "Don't drag your feet," she says, trying to set me right. "You're too big, kiddo, you're taller than me." I shake my head, slip to my knees, and lie dramatically across the kitchen floor like a damsel in distress. "Come on, ham, get up."

"Mommy!" I whine, lifting my arms for her. She steps over my body and looks in Grandpa's old room.

"Where's Lyla?" She brought Lyla back home last week. She had a shiner. She's hardly said two words to me except, "Get out of my way."

"I don't know. Out." I drop my arms.

"Do you want an omelet?" She rummages through the onion and fruit bowl and pulls out some potatoes with small green stems. Science experiments. UFOs. "And home fries? I can put onion and bell pepper in them and . . ." she opens the fridge, "mushrooms and cheddar in the omelet. I'll eat one too."

"Yes," I say.

"Come on, get up, the floor is dirty. You're not a baby."

"I am a baby."

"I have news for you, girlie."

"Fine."

"Did you go to class today?" she asks, starting to cut onion and bell pepper.

"Yeah."

"And?"

"Actually, something weird happened." I slump in the kitchen chair, lay my head in my arms, against the table.

"Okay, tell me. Also, sit up, don't be a slouch."

"Ms. Lavoi my English teacher thinks I'm smart."

"You are smart."

"Yeah, well I think I'm her new cause célèbre."

Mom huffs and looks at me. "Counting your chickens before they've hatched perhaps?"

"Gee, thanks."

"Oh stop, you know I think you can make it. Have you sent those head shots out?"

"No," I sigh.

"Nicole, I spent two hundred dollars on those things. It's a phone book, open it, start mailing."

"I know."

"Have you called that agent back? What's the one, the one that Marla uses?"

"No."

She sets the knife down and looks serious. I avert my eyes. "Listen, last year you came to me and said this was important to you. You asked for my support. I gave you the gym membership, which I know you don't use, I gave you the money for those head shots which have been sitting in that box for close to a year, I let you sign up for that class on the Westside, with, with, that cult leader, whatever his name is!" She raises the knife.

"He's a Scientologist not a cult leader."

"Oh lord."

"I'm not a drone, okay? I'm not going to become a Scientologist. Jesus."

"From your lips to God's ears."

"It was a boring class anyway. It didn't help like I thought it would."

"I'm taking a leap of faith here based on your promise that you would try, that this meant something to you."

"I know."

"And what do you do? You chop your hair up and cover your face like a common chola. We're better than that. You're better than that."

"Oh, we're *so* much better."

"We are. You aren't like those girls."

"What am I like?"

"What is happening, mija? What is going on with you?"

"Nothing. I don't know. I don't want to talk about this. I just want to eat and be with you."

She turns around and finishes cutting. Olive oil sizzles in the pan, smoke moves toward the ceiling where I watch it form shapes from below.

×

Tori Amos is a revolutionary. Marijuana wipes my brain clean. I drag the glue stick against the journal page and press a picture of Paul Newman into the cardboard, smoothing the edges. There is a knock at the window and

I lift my head. There is another knock, this time louder, I walk over and pull back the curtain.

"Puta, let me in!" hisses Chelo.

"Why don't you go to the front door?" I ask, making a weird face at her.

She shrugs. "Meh, I'm already here."

"Whatever, Romeo." I open the window and she crawls inside. "You're stepping on my mom's hydrangea," I say, pulling her over.

"Oh, sorry." She looks behind her into the flower bed. "What time is it?" she asks, brushing leaves off her sweater.

"How should I know? You're the one who just crawled in here."

"Don't you have a clock?"

"Yeah," I say, checking the digital on my dresser. "It's one thirty. What are you doing, man?"

"I dunno," she shrugs, "I was bored. Can't sleep. You're awake."

"Yeah but I'm in my own house."

"Man, you're just always a bitch aren't you? Like all the time? Even at like," she cranes her neck dramatically and looks at the digital clock, "1:36. Fine I'll go." She turns around, heading back onto the windowsill.

"What are you talking about, man? Use the door, first of all, and like, I just, what are you doing here? I just, wasn't expecting you is all."

"Let's go for a drive."

"Right now? You're crazy."

"Why not?"

"I dunno. Where would we go?"

"Let's go to the mountains."

"Like, what? Altadena or something?"

"Yeah."

I look at my journal, half-collaged, half-finished thoughts, empty pages, waiting for me to fill them up.

"Okay, fuck it," I say, grabbing my jeans and hoodie. "Let's go."

"Yes!" says Chelo, smiling. "I love you man, you are, like, the coolest all the time."

"I thought I was a bitch."

"You are, but you're always down. I dunno, you're both, somehow."

×

We push the seats back in my car and look out the scratched plastic sunroof. The stars twinkle and shine down on us. I can smell wood burning and know that one of the rich houses below has a fire going. The earth is warm tinder and grass. Moisture and light.

"You just seem so sure of yourself." She passes the one hitter and the lighter, I reach over and grab them, not taking my eyes off the sky.

"Does it seem that way?" A shooting star races through the night. My eyes follow it until it disappears behind a tree.

"Yes," she says simply.

"I'm not."

"I know," she answers. "It just seems that way."

"What are you going to do?"

"Fuck, I don't know. I used to think I'd go to college and get out like that but fuck, we fucked that up, didn't we?"

I turn my head toward her and blink. My chest hollowing out. "I guess I hadn't thought about it."

"What are you going to do?" she asks, moving her arm in waves.

"I don't know."

"You thought you were going to get into Harvard or something? You have shittier grades than I do. I'm surprised they haven't kicked you out."

"Stop. I can't think about it."

"You'll figure it out," she says, sounding slightly more sympathetic.

"You will too, Chelo, you're smart."

"I think I'm going to apply to Otis."

"Oh yeah?"

"Yeah. The deadline hasn't passed. Mr. Gotto thinks I have a chance."

"You're going to be okay."

A bird, a whip-poor-will perhaps, a night bird, sounds around us, the echo of our words, the bright, clean taste of ash, we're pulled into the navy, star-spotted sky, covered in blue.

"I know."

×

Chelo nudges me and I open my eyes. "Hey," she says, groggy. We fell asleep and now the birds are different birds, or the same, just singing morning songs. "We passed out. That shit must have been indica."

"Yeah, or we came out here at two a.m."

"What time is it?"

I turn the key and the dash lights up 10:47. "Fuck!" I shout, pushing my hair back. "I'm on probation, I'm gonna get kicked out!"

"No you're not, relax." Chelo's language is so much smoother, softer, feminine in the morning. I look at her and all her eyeliner has smudged, her acne scars a little pinker.

"We need to go now. You said so last night, you're surprised they haven't kicked me out."

She looks at me sadly. I turn the car off and fall back into my reclined chair and start to cry quietly, not dramatic or anything, just a soft morning drizzle, and she lets me. I rub her Felix the Cat key chain, focusing on his yellow bag of magic tricks. The cold hard edge of the car keys. She pulls the weed out from her front hoodie pocket and flips the dash, takes the pipe and passes it. All this moonshine and dreams of things I don't understand, swilling my daybreak. I take the pipe and cover the carb, watch her exhale, the dew cascading in small rivulets against the glass, smudging up the clean outdoors, but just through what I'm looking at, not through anything real. Outside, when the door opens, the world is still the same bright place.

×

I'm dodging squirrels toward the bus stop on Lake when an olive green 1960s Lotus pulls up beside me. I stop walking and squint into the glare of the tinted window. It was tinted in the late 1970s and is actually just an appliqué sticker with hundreds of gradating black dots blurring into one solid mass. I used to pull on it as a child.

"Hi," says the voice, disinterested, revealing itself. Black-tinted Ray-Bans and Montecito Car Club baseball hat. Slowly the glasses are removed and I see him. I tilt my head and wipe sweat from my brow. I'm aware suddenly that my tits are hanging out through the large rips of my shirt. I have drawn hearts and dotted lines for slicing, and various X marks the spot smudges on my arms, including the star tattoo I got last summer on the inside of my wrist. Peeling Wite-Out on my fingernails. He doesn't say anything, leans across the seat, and pops my lock. I open the door and slide into the soft, butter-yellow leather. He rolls up the window to keep the AC in. The cold air hits my face like delicious kisses. It's winter but LA is melting. The smell of the interior is at once familiar and newly desirable. My fingers grip the polished oak and I remember how much I love money. How much I take refuge in the fact that at the end of the day I am his daughter. It all washes off. Nothing a good haircut, day in the sun, and some nice clothes can't fix. My place is always waiting.

San Gabriel Valley, LA City girl. Honored, educated, old, and California blue. My grandmother can make paella, enchiladas, and Spanish rice. She is French, Dutch. We are blond, we are lanky, we are athletic, we are philanthropic, we are smart, and we get what we want. At the end of the day I will always be Nicole Felicia Darling, if you do or don't please.

My grandfather tells me in his old-man way that I am a daily reminder of my father's failures. That I am the only good thing to come of them. I am somehow always the best and worst thing to happen to my father. It is a thing they feel completely comfortable telling me. As if announcing the gazpacho was meant to be served chilled. Spoiled, sensitive, apathetic, mean, narcissistic. A righteous, moral man. The most socially honorable man I've ever known. The only man I know to do great good and evil in the name of progress. He is loyal only to the oath of human justice. Poor dad.

Asshole. Shitty excuse maker.

The first to offer himself in the name of the greater good. As a child, I watched as he routinely stopped his car in traffic to help someone with a flat tire. I saw him break up a fight between two men in the parking lot of a restaurant, pull a knife away from one man, and throw it into the road. He donated my first-communion dress, teddy bear, and Pound Puppy pajamas to a children's center raising money for flood victims. "There's always someone worse off than you, don't ya forget." The only hands he bites are the ones that love him.

He looks at me when I shut the door, and starts driving toward the house.

"Where are we going?" I ask.

"Back home, you need to change."

"Why? What for?"

"We're driving to Palm Desert, your grandfather wants to see me. I thought we could go together."

"When did you get in?"

"Yesterday morning. I'm staying with your uncle in Marina del Rey," he says, meaning the boat.

"Oh."

"What's wrong with you?" He squints at me.

"What do you mean?" I ask, looking down, knowing what he means but wishing that I didn't.

"Your mother lets you dress like that?"

"You let my mother raise me. Who says I want to go with you?"

"You don't want to?"

"No, that's not what I said."

"Come on, we'll have a nice afternoon. We can do sushi afterwards, you and I. The Ai, what about it?"

"Lyla's here."

He slows the car and pulls over a few houses away from ours. "Really?" he asks quietly.

"Yeah."

"Shit." He taps the steering wheel with his thumb. "She's home?" I shrug and he scans the road as if looking for something out there, as if the answer will dart in front of the car.

"What's the problem if she is?"

"Nothing. Nothing," he says under his breath.

"Something about her boyfriend. Mom drove up and got her last week."

"Is she okay?"

"I don't know, man," I say, growing agitated. "Can I, like, go?"

He pulls a bitch and we head back toward the freeway. "Target's open. You just need a new shirt, everything else looks fine."

I slouch out and he hands me his credit card through the window. "And wash your arms." He grabs my hand and turns it over. I see him see the star tattoo and brace myself. He drags his thumb across it lightly. "What tiny wrists you have," he whispers, and lets go.

×

My grandfather sits in a white tennis suit with purple and turquoise lightning stripes across the ankles. The gold plastic rim of his visor glints in my eyes. The court is bright and the air is hot and dry. I can feel sweat drip from my armpits slowly down my breasts and along my rib cage.

"Nicole," he says from the side of the court where he's drinking a scotch on the rocks in a crystal tumbler. In the distance the fronds of two thin palms wiggle their fingers in what feels like imaginary breeze.

I walk toward him and he motions to my father. "Alex," he says, pointing at me, "give her the racket." My dad's face turns stormy and he walks toward me and hands it over. I hold it awkwardly and watch as my father turns and starts for the bright-green lawn beyond us and toward the condo. "Where are you going?" asks my grandfather, his lips pursed and unpleased.

"To lie down," my father says. "It's too hot." My grandpa makes a sour face and looks at me again saying nothing. He reaches out and grabs my wrist.

"Loosen up." I do as he instructs and he taps my wrist lightly, almost a smack. "That's too loose."

"What am I trying for?"

"Trying for?" he asks, confused. "Because it's something to do."

"No, I mean, what is the desired looseness?"

"Desired?" His expression changes to one of confusion. I have confused him again, with my words.

"What am I going for?" He still says nothing. "How tight should I hold the racket?" I ask, taking a final approach.

"Hold it like you want to hit the ball."

"Sounds easy enough."

"If it were easy you would have done it by now."

Back at the condo my grandmother arranges tulips in a tall, ceramic art deco vase. My dad is outside sitting by the pool. I can see him check his watch. He looks bored. I sit on the peach couch with the floral pattern that I've loved since I was a girl. Gently tugging at the plastic stitching that forms the flowers. My grandmother closes the sliding glass door and my dad becomes a blurry figure.

"I'm going to make some sandwiches," she says. "Would you like one? Egg salad."

"No, thank you." I say, even though I'm hungry. I hate

egg salad. The only thing here that I like is this couch. I even hate the pool. As a girl, my sister hit her head on the lip of concrete near the diving board and almost drowned. My grandfather accused her of doing it on purpose to make a scene. I remember a thin plume of her blood like ink from an octopus, or watercolor from the tip of a paintbrush dipped into a cup, expanding from her hair as my dad fished her out. I sat on this couch watching *ET* and decided not to go swimming in it ever again.

My dad takes off his loafers and stands on the first two steps leading into the shallow end. He looks behind him toward the house then walks out and toward us. He holds his loafers in his right hand and opens the sliding door with his left.

"Come on," he says, "it's time to go." So I stand and we leave.

Driving back home on the 5 we're quiet. I watch the duck farm as we approach the 57. I think about Raging Waters and summer camp. How I used to pretend I was sick each Tuesday, field trip day, because I couldn't count the money that my mother stuffed into my fanny pack and was too embarrassed to ask a counselor to help me buy lunch. When I did go on the weekly field trips and it was time for lunch break I knew that a ten-dollar bill would cover the counting change part. But one time the cashier stopped me. "You need thirty-five cents," said the teenage girl beneath the imposter Hot Dog on a Stick hat. Her hair was shaggy and fell across the side of her face in a hair sprayed swoop. She wore a Swatch. Normally I would have handed her another dollar, but I didn't have any dollar bills left. Thirty-five cents felt like such an unfathomable number to gather up from the cup of my hands. Terror swirled in my chest. Large and small and different-sized coins. "Don't you know how to count thirty-five cents?" My eyes welled up with tears and before I could answer she huffed, blew her bangs out of her eyes and reached over the counter, scooping a quarter and dime from my hands. "Here," she said, passing the red-and-white-striped, oil-spotted box of chicken strips and fries. "Straws are over there." She nodded toward the napkin table and handed me a Coke.

"How are you?" he asks, seven hours into our time together.

I blink and turn away from the window. "When I was little and we lived out here, there was a mountain, or, well, I thought it was a mountain, and there was this sort of intricate pulley system, it was like Mouse Trap, this thing looked like the Zipper at the carnival, anyway, it scooped up rocks then dumped them someplace else beneath the ground. I could never see where, really." He doesn't say anything and I see that he's furrowed his brow, which has sprouted the lines of annoyance. I've swum too far again. "Anyway, the mountain, it's gone now."

"The rock quarry. You didn't live out here that long."

"That's not what I meant."

"What did you mean?"

"Nothing. I just was thinking out loud."

"You should pay attention to that. Someone could misconstrue your out-loud thoughts for passive-aggression. Your mother is passive-aggressive."

"I don't understand."

"It will benefit you in this life to be direct."

"I wasn't trying to passive-aggressively accuse you of anything. If I wanted to say you were a crap dad for making us live out here while you were living in Hawaii I would have just said that."

"How quickly you feel implicated."

"Why can't you just be normal? I only meant I thought it was a mountain and now I realize it was just a pile of rocks."

"What do you think a mountain is?"

"How's school?"

"Shitty!" I say, starting to cry.

He pulls across three lanes of traffic and exits beside a Denny's. "Why can't *I* be normal? You look like Elvira! Why am I getting frantic phone calls from your mother telling me she hasn't seen you in forty-eight hours?"

"Is that why you're here?"

"What do you think?"

"I don't know!" I scream, getting out of the car. I stop and walk back to the window, which is now rolled down. "No one tells me anything!"

"That's bullshit. Quit being dramatic, get back in here."

I open the door and sit back down.

"Here," he says, offering me an old Starbucks napkin from the glove compartment.

"How come I have to be the one to figure everything

out? It's like everything with you people is a game of Clue and as soon as shit seems normal, one of you assholes changes the rules again. Why can't you just say, 'I heard you were missing and I'm worried about you'? Me, indirect? That's a laugh. You're the most confusing, indirect person I know. You're like some angry philosopher who smoked too much bad stuff. Ya know?"

"Don't speak to me like you're Moon Zappa."

"Who?!"

"Frank Zappa's . . . it doesn't matter."

"You're so prehistoric and you don't even know it."

"Nicole, I don't know what to tell you. I try to see you girls, you say no. I don't come, your mother puts me through hell."

"Why do you listen to me? Why can't you just come?"

"I try to respect your wishes."

"I'm sixteen! You don't want to come."

He's quiet and grabs a toothpick from the center console. "Are you hungry?"

"No." I wipe at my face. "I'm always crying in cars with guys."

"I'm not a guy, I'm your father."

"I know." And then I just give up. I don't know what I'm trying to say anyway and who gives a fuck really.

×

What if I stopped here to tell you something else was coming? Something on the horizon? Sometimes I have these lucid feelings as if everything is being shown to me on some supercomputer from the future. Or the way I imagine death is, where your life flashes before your eyes. I know that's cliché, but things line up that way. I know how I might appear on the outside, withdrawn, maybe rotten and spoiled, perhaps a little pulled back and reserved but the truth is I am alive, full of passion, and, most of all, as I age slowly on this crumbling and dissolving planet, full of sadness. I am sad. It drips like muck over my eyeballs, like the black goo on *The X-Files*, and the way Mulder knows the goo is coming for him. He knows because he can sense it. I can sense things all the time. I feel like Virginia Woolf's Orlando looking out at the future, you and the future me, and I can't shake this feeling that this sadness will be the thing I'll have to fight the rest of my life, and that love is like this mirage, a stupid dump of water in a wrinkling, ripply distance. I know instinctually that I will spend my entire life thirsty as fuck running for something always just out of reach. This hallway is an endless eternity and my locker is all I have and my books will never fit and my lock will always jam and the spaces around the bodies of my peers are outlined in light and I can't escape this shadow.

×

The little Scantron is sweaty underneath my fingers and I chew the eraser at the bottom of the pencil. I hold it above the word *other*. I look up at the nurse behind the counter, the one who handed me the clipboard and papers. *Pacific Islander* makes me smirk. I fill in *Hispanic* then quickly rub it out. I've hovered above the question awhile now. I stand and walk toward the window, she looks up, "Finished?"

"No. Not quite. I was wondering if I could leave this section blank?" I hold out the clipboard and point at the race question.

"No, I'm afraid not," she says looking up with an *I'm sorry* face. "That's how we keep track of who's using our facility."

"You give this information out?"

"Not to the general public but Planned Parenthood is a government-subsidized program, so yes, we have to keep track of how many women use our facility."

"Men don't use the facility?" Now she smirks at me, I've revealed myself somehow as a rabble-rouser, some sort of smart aleck.

"Yes, of course men are allowed to use our facility, but in general, our services pertain to women. Just fill out the Caucasian option and you should be fine."

"I'm not Caucasian."

"Then fill out whichever option best pertains to your ethnicity, return the forms, and I'll call you when the next available nurse is ready."

"Okay, thank you." I turn around and leave the clipboard on the magazine table, resting on a pile of issues of *People* and *Scientific American*, below the cheaply framed photo of a whale diving into the neon-painted ocean, alive with brightly shining fish and coral. I push open the door, and sunshine and fast food smells of South Lake hit my nostrils. I hop the steps and make my way toward the Orean health-food shack to grab a fizzy green drink.

I walk to the pay phone on the corner, sucking the already empty Styrofoam cup, and drop in fifty cents. It rings a few times until Chelo answers.

"Hello?"

"Hey, it's me."

"Where are you calling from?"

"A pay phone. Look, what are you doing?"

"My parents are fighting with Adel so I'm taking Ugly to the mall. Wanna come?"

"No, I'm in Pasadena and don't have cash. Gotta wait till my mom gets home to get more."

"You sure? I could lend you some money if you can get here, for the ride back. I pinched forty from my dad's bag this morning. We're going to the Hello Kitty store and I'm taking her to Claire's to get her ears pierced."

"No, it's cool, I'm not good with little kids."

"How do you know?"

"I don't know, maybe I am, I'm just sort of, I think I'm gonna stay close to home."

"Okay," she says, I can see her shrug, "suit yourself. See you at school tomorrow?"

"Maybe."

"Fool you're gonna get kicked out."

"Maybe."

"All right James Dean, smell you later."

"Smell ya." I hang up and walk back toward home.

I open the front door and the house is cool and shady. Walk to my mother's room and push open the door. I sit on the edge of the bed. Parsley is asleep. I pull him into my lap and stroke his head, he nuzzles into my touch.

"I tried to get birth control today. No, I'm not having sex yet, but you know, I just thought it's better to be prepared for when I do.

"No, I wouldn't say they were rude, they were really nice actually. She asked me a few uncomfortable questions but overall it ended up being a positive experience.

"I walked, it's just around the corner you know. Well, you make a good point, I could have been sore after the exam but I wasn't, it's not so bad you know. I've had it done before. I took myself. It's just around the corner. I'm not sure what's for dinner. Whatever you feel like making is fine with me. Let's see, I don't think so, *Facts of Life* starts at two, I think it's still noon, we have a few hours. Of course I don't mind making you a sandwich, what kind would you like? Tuna? Of course, I might make one myself.

"I did see them, they're beautiful, you're such a wonderful florist. Those assholes are lucky to have you." Parsley wrestles free and slips away.

"No, I don't mind. I don't have to eat either. I can just come back another time, or you just let me know when you're free." The pillow is soft and my head slips into its shape. I reach my hand across the bed and touch his tail, it falls away and branch shadows flutter above, the wings of birds beating on their limbs, the outside shimmering across the wall. Damp circles form their gullies around my temples and I turn my head, wipe away tears, and move my hands blindly, searching for a dry spot of land.

"It's easy," says Jessica, pulling her boobs into a dark purple tube top in front of my mirror. "I can't believe it only took you an entire semester to invite me over. It's nice here." She looks around my grease stain of a room. "I like the bedspread." She smacks her gum. "I bet tons of hot guys are gonna be there. I mean, can you imagine?" She smiles at herself, fluffs her hair, and turns and grabs my arms and squeals.

"No," I answer and touch her boobs. But not in a sexy way, and she gets this.

"No what?"

"No, I can't imagine. Can you, Yoko?"

Jessica laughs nervously and rolls her eyes. "You're a weirdo sometimes?"

"Am I?" I ask, quickly lifting my eyebrows up and down like Groucho Marx.

"Yeah, a real A-plus weirdo. Stop it, you're being creepy. Move."

She pushes me out of the way and grabs my lipstick. I flop backward onto the bed. "You think someone there will talk to me?"

"What are you talking about, duh. You're such a Betty."

"I'm a regular Betty Poop!" I shout and shoot up in place like Dracula, baring my fangs and claws at her.

"No seriously, don't act like a nerd. I will go home."

"Fuck you, man."

"Fuck you!"

"I'm just being me or whatever."

"Oh boo-hoo, get dressed."

"I am dressed, geez," I say, sitting up regular. "I'm into this, what's wrong with it?"

"You look like a dyke."

"So?"

"So you're not a dyke. Put on one of your cool vintage dresses."

"No, man, I want to wear my Dickieeeeeeeees!" and I say this like my voice is a tiny helium rocket in a parking lot, heading for the sky. "Besides my boobs look good in this." I tug on the bottom of the wifebeater. If nothing else I have great tits. Oh yeah, I've got giant tits. "I did my hair and makeup. God, you're such a Hitler."

"I'm Jewish."

"I know! You never shut up about it."

"You never talk unless it's to say something bitchy or weird."

"Okay, fine. Tell me how to snag a hottie."

"So it's easy. You see some scam-worthy babe and you saddle up sort of like, cool, you know? And just be like, 'Hey, I'm Nikki,' you know?"

"I guess."

"You really are a Betty, despite your total lack of sociability. You should be like, hospitalized or something, like, that book in class, *Girl Interrup*—"

And then she interrupts herself, sets down my lipstick. "I'm sorry."

"It's okay. It's a good book." And now I regret telling

her. It happened in a moment of stoned weakness. She asked about my sister and so I told her. I've never even told Chelo and it's a real thing that I regret. Talk about not choosing wisely, Indiana.

"I know, I just, I'm sorry."

"Look it's cool. Do you want me to grab a knife and, like, freak out on you?"

"God no."

"Okay, so it's cool."

"Okay." And she turns around again and looks at herself again and again, and again, and again, never once seeing who she is.

×

Dan is on the orange couch, Melissa Flores sitting in his lap. They're both holding red plastic cups and talking to Ian and Sam. Sam has just returned from New York where he was visiting his father, some sort of big-deal art collector. Everyone's been kissing his ass all week, trying to see if he got laid or something menial like that. Dan sees me and looks away. I head into the kitchen and try to find an unopened beer on the sticky overcrowded countertop.

"Nice dress," says a deep unfamiliar voice. I turn around. It's Joey Kandarian, from orchestra. He's broad in the soldiers, tall, beefy around the middle, and dressed like a Rude Boy. His two-tones are worn in and sort of tattered, he keeps readjusting his Buddy Holly opticals and looking at me like he just ate something bad and now he's not sure about it. His greasy brown hair falling from his pomp into his face.

"Thanks, I got it on Melrose." I spot a Corona behind a half-empty bottle of lemon Tequiza and snatch for it.

"Here." He grabs it first and pops it for me. "You're in musical theater, right?"

"Just theater," I say, casually.

"Yeah but you're in musical theater, you practice in our building. I've heard you sing."

"Yeah, well, it's more like an elective."

"No it's not. It's a department."

"Okay so what?" I ask, taking a swallow and looking into the living room.

"You have a nice voice," he says following my gaze.

"Oh. Thanks." Go away. Go away. Go away.

"Do you read music?"

"Sure, got to, don't you?"

"Totally."

"I'm a better actor."

"Yeah?"

"Totally. I'm getting an agent, you know? I mean, I've practically got one right now, actually." I look away from him, like someone better is out there, waiting. Take a swig.

"Now or after graduation?"

"Now, duh! I've already been in some stuff. I model. Are you in a band or something?"

"I'm in orchestra," he says simply. I shuck corn. I'm in orchestra. I sell car insurance. I'm in orchestra. I like beer and peanuts. I'm in orchestra.

"I know but . . . I mean, outside of school."

"I mostly just hang out, I guess."

"Well I'm busy, like a lot, trying to do this thing, ya know?" I take another swallow and tap my fingers against the wall.

"Well, it was nice talking to you."

"Totes McTotes." I turn my head and look back into the living room. He leaves and I sigh, walk toward the backyard where Mike is smoking a J and talking to some older kids I've never met.

"Oh, hey," he says smiling real big and dopey. He reaches his arm out for me and lurches slightly. I quicken my step to sort of catch him, but also to be there so he can catch me. It's seamless and only I can tell it almost went another way. I like that we have secrets. He looks up and tugs on my puffy sleeve. This stupid dress. "Pretty," he says, sort of sloppy. "Hey, Jules, this is Nikki."

"Hey," says the beautiful slightly older girl in the hot-pink X-Girl jumper with patterns of houses and small ferns covering it. Her black hair has been cut into a Louise Brooks bob and her nails are the familiar lacquered red of the hot girls who hang out at the Dresden.

"Jules hangs out at Jabberjaw. That's where we met."

"What's Jabberjaw? Is that like a rave? Like JuJu Beats? I'm not a raver, I told you that." Jabberjaw is the coolest club in town and I've never been let in. It's sort of dingy and like a bombed-out hole-in-the-wall. Drew Barrymore hangs out there.

"It's a club," says Jules shortly. She stands from where she's been sitting on the stucco wall, stubs out her

142

American Spirit, and blows her smoke in my face then walks away.

"What's up her culo?"

"You're cute," says Mike sarcastically. The last few weeks he's been testy with me and I'm not sure why.

"Why are you hanging out at Jabberjoke? That place is filled with zombies."

"Oh yeah, you're not jealous at all."

"Fine, then invite me, I'd go."

"Okay, but you'd need to act like an adult. Not like a brat. I saw Drew Barrymore there a few weeks ago, with Eric Erlandson, you know, from Hole?"

"Hole, what's that, like a band?"

He rolls his eyes. I'm quiet and look out into the yard, or the world. I love Drew Barrymore. I don't know what to do. Why is he being mean? He's never been mean, just high. I talk because he listens. Not because I don't care. Maybe I should complain less. Ask how he is doing more. I think about all the ways I can try to feel different and none of them seem wise or viable. "Do you feel like you're never saying anything?"

"Someone left Nietzsche's greatest hits at the bus stop?"

"What?"

"Never mind. What's wrong?"

"Nothing."

"Everything," he says, teasingly, but really I don't like being teased and I didn't say anything funny. Joey Kandarian walks by and smiles. I let out a moan and bury my face in my hands.

I stop by Mike's house early the next day. "Did you have fun last night?" I ask, standing in the doorway to the garage. He's playing video games and smoking a J and looks up startled, but then composes himself and looks bored.

"It was okay." He shrugs. "How'd you sneak in?"

"There is literally no fence around your house. Your door is open. I heard music."

He shrugs. Finally sets down the console and looks at me. "So what's up? Why have you come to my garage of broken dreams and condoms?"

"Why do you do that?" I ask, sitting down. "Insult yourself."

"Oh, don't be so righteous all the time. What does it say about you that you always think I'm being serious? I don't need you to babysit my feelings. If I wanted to be policed I'd leave the house." And this shuts me up. He stands and walks to the clothing rack. He's shirtless as usual and in a pair of boxer shorts. Sexy coffee colored. He takes a drag of the joint and stubs it out in the 1950s copper cowboy hat ashtray.

"I'm sorry," he says, bowing gallantly before me, as if my servant. "Please speak. How dare I make a fool of the sensitive young darling, Darling."

"Did I do something to you?"

"No," he answers, turning away quickly and grabbing a shirt. "I'm in a bad mood. It's my mother's birthday, okay? You can psychoanalyze me later."

"I'm really sorry," I say genuinely and then I'm quiet.

"God, don't be such a martyr. It's better I tell you this now, before it haunts you into your twenties, but you can be real insufferable sometimes."

"Why are you being such a bitch?"

"You don't hang with me because you feel sorry for me, do you?"

"What? No way. How could you even ask me that?" I hang with you because you're beautiful and I see your soul and you have good musicals and a VCR and weed and cool clothes and tell me about stuff I've never heard of before like the B-52's *Wild Planet*. I hang with you because I'm in love with you. "Can I buy you Denny's?"

"Case in point. Insufferable response. But yes. Only I want to go to the really old one out in San Bernardino, past the Ren Faire."

"Off the 605?"

"Yes."

"It'll take us forever to get there."

"I can drive."

"No, it's okay. I've got my mom's car. Let's go."

"Okay," he says quietly, pulling on his pants. "Thank you, but let's get high first."

×

He's quiet on the ride and fiddles with the stations, trying to find a tune. Finally he settles on "Edge of Seventeen" and leans back, wraps his vintage OP shirt around his head like a blindfold, and loops his arms across his chest.

"Are you going to sleep?"

"Well, not exactly," he says, pulling the shirt up so I can see him. "This is a car. I'm resting my eyes."

"Oh."

"Why?" He coughs into his fist and moves his butt around like a cat trying to get comfortable.

"I don't know. You don't want to talk?"

"I knew it!" he says, sitting up. "You did come over to tell me something. I could *sense* it." He rips the shirt off and smiles like a demented loon.

"God, so what?"

"We always talk about you!"

"Dude, that's so not true! I'm surprised you remember anything we talk about, you're high all the time."

"Fine, you want to talk. Let's talk. Is it about trying to make me feel shitty for being gay and not wanting to fuck you?"

"God, no! Why are you being so terrible?"

"Because my mom is dead and it's her birthday and all you ever want to talk about are boys and crummy existential shit I just don't care to listen to anymore."

"Okay, fine." I turn the radio up and he turns toward the window, balls up his shirt, and uses it as a pillow against the glass.

"I'm not your personal therapist, okay, your boring straight-girl gay monkey sidekick, okay?" The windows fog around his mouth. "Man, you were such a little bitch last night. You really pissed off Jules."

"Okay, okay, I get it. I embarrassed you in front of your cool friend. I'm sorry. Look, I'm really trying to be nice to you right now but you're making it really freaking hard.

However you have made a good point and I will try harder in the future to be less self-centered."

He doesn't say anything and moves his shoulders against the seat. I look to the left at the mountains. I have always lived in the shadow of them, looming dry and brown, moss green and white tipped, hawk circled and majestic, sitting always to my back, holding me.

"I talk about other things besides boys."

He groans and sticks his fingers in his ears. "You are being really rotten! My mom is dead. Dead mom."

I don't say anything, roll down the window. "Can I have a cigarette?"

Finally he sighs. "I wish I could tape-record you. Only you would complain about how no one wants to date you when the best-looking guy at school is tripping all over himself to sniff your cat."

"What are you even talking about?"

"Your little dirty friend Dan. Have you looked at him?"

"Oh god. He is not trying to get with me."

Mike groans. "I can't listen to you anymore!"

"And he's not the best-looking guy at school. You are."

He shakes his head and sighs, covers his face again.

We drive silently for about ten minutes. I see a 76 station and pull off the freeway. San Bernardino is all around us. I feel big-city girl, I feel obvious. "Hey," I say, nudging him. "We're in San Berdoo, get up."

"That was fast. I feel like I just closed my eyes."

"You did. Oh wow. That guy has boots on, like the cowboy kind."

Mike rubs his eyes. "Don't be such a Clay," he says,

meaning *Less Than Zero*. "Here." He holds out five bucks and I wave it away.

"It's cool."

There's a paper sign out front written with sharpie, advertising homemade jerky. I pull the glass door open, a little bell above my head rings, and in the distance, beyond the 76, through the register window, I see the emblem of Circle K and sigh relieved. Civilization. I'll stop there on the way home for road snacks. *Strange things are afoot.*

All two sets of eyes are on me. An older guy, maybe in his twenties, dressed in baggy jeans and a black Raiders jersey, wearing white tube socks and chanclas, a pair of black sunglasses pushed back on his Brylled-up hair, glistening blue. His hands have dots and teardrops in the creases between his thumb and forefinger. He follows me to the counter.

There's a rack of *Teen Angels* magazines behind the register, near the cigarettes.

"Ten on five," I say, handing over the money. Some zitty kid, twenty maybe, a blond side part and old-fashioned checkered-style cowboy shirt buttoned at the cuffs. Except it isn't old, it says Joe Boxer on the chest pocket. Walmart cowboy.

"You from around here?" asks Chanclas.

"No," I say as chill as I can, I tilt my head back just enough to show I'm not afraid but not a threat. And of course, as soon as I do, feel epically stupid.

"You white? What are you?" he asks.

"Mexican and white. Yeah."

"Shit," he says leaning back and laughing, he aw-shucks his arm and swats the air with an open hand. Real funny guy. "Man, that is far out." He looks at me steady this time. We're both stoned. He knows I know, and I try to pretend like I don't, but I do. He insists on our druggy familiarity. "You're real fine girl. I like your hair and makeup. Where y'all from?" *Y'all.*

"Los Angeles."

"Shit, I knew," he says. "It's all over your face. Yeah, got a brother out in Carson. My daughter lives in Montebello."

"Cool," I say, backing away.

"Hey, get home safe," he says. "It's a long way back."

×

"Who was that vato you were making friends with?" asks Mike, taking the bag of gummies from my hand as I slide back in and start the engine.

"Some weird hick cholo. But he was really nice."

"Cholos are always nice," he says matter-of-factly. "I never met a mean cholo, you?"

"No, I guess not."

"My uncle's a cholo." He shoves gummies into his mouth. "He lives in Whittier."

"Oh yeah?"

"Yeah. And he's never said a mean thing to me once and I'm a baby fag."

I head toward the dense green of the woods, Moons Over My Hammy beckoning, and we ascend.

×

Mike picks up the menu and flips it around. "Where's hash browns?" he asks incredulously.

"Here, look. Under late-night snacks."

"That's insane. It's a breakfast food."

I shrug.

"Doesn't that bother you?" he asks, and it shakes me into the moment.

"I'm sorry, what?" I look up, sounding like my father.

"Don't you think it's dumb that hash browns are on the stoner snack menu? Mozzarella sticks, sure, but fucking hash browns? What the hell?"

I set down my menu and look at him. Really, really look at him.

"What?" he asks raising his shoulders.

"I can't decide if you are or you aren't."

"I am or I am not what?" he asks, screwing up his face.

"For real. Sometimes I can't tell if you're for real."

"What the hell does that mean?"

"It means I think you say shit just to fuck with me."

"Oh you get real," he says, relaxing and tossing the menu on the table. "I thought you were going to say some *for real* shit. Earth to Nikki." He picks up his straw and taps my head with it. "Not. Everything. Is. About. You. I thought we just went over this. I could smoke another bowl though." He looks out the window toward the car.

"After," I say.

"Let's get it to go," he says. "Let's eat it in the mountains."

I laugh. "Seriously?"

"Yes."

"Okay."

"Cool." And he nods. "That would make me feel good."

"Then it's done," I say. "Consider it done."

×

Mike's got the steamy plastic trays in his lap and my mom's old Aerostar moans and scuttles over the loose rock that has fallen into the twisty road, tall fir trees jutting along the side. The entire San Berdoo and IE below us. *It's ten p.m. do you know where your children are?*

"Ohmigod!" he shouts, craning his neck out the window. "Look! It's fucking Raging Waters."

I idle and turn my head. A giant net, like the kind in Vietnam movies, or *M*A*S*H*, flaps in the distance, attached to two long poles shooting hundreds of feet into the sky. "That's a stupid golf course. Raging Waters is way, way behind us."

"Oh." And he pulls himself back in. "Oh, up there!" he shouts again, pointing in the distance at a little pull-off. "Let's eat there."

"Okay," I say, heading toward it.

We park and get out, walk to the edge of the overhang. It is a beautiful thing, wide-open free-fall space, houses, swimming pools, trees, and smog. There's hawk screeching and the quiet scurry of animals. I kick my feet, and small pebbles and sediment fall into the emptiness below. Mike pops the lids and the sweet smell of syrup hits my nose. I grab one of my sausage links, dip it in the syrup cup, and munch. It's salty, sweet, and warm. Mike unwraps the little plastic spoons and forks and squirts ketchup on his hash browns. He spoons large bites into his mouth, wiping away little crumbs already on his lips.

"Sorry I was mean earlier," he says, looking down at his food and dumping a packet of pepper on his scrambled eggs.

I shrug. "It's true, I talk too much about myself." He puts an arm around my shoulder and pulls me close and I stiffen.

"Is this weird?" he asks, meaning the hug.

"No." I shake my head and hug back.

×

At school on Monday I am feeling good, jolly. And I don't want to see anyone. I decide to wake up early and go to class. I shower and brush my hair into its proper bob, not letting it dry all fizzy-wisp curly-brains. I set it, sit on the toilet, flip through a copy of my mother's newest issue of *Sunset*. At school, I park near the stairs, so I don't drag my feet thinking before I ascend. I grab the handrail and walk myself up, one clippety-clip at a time. I'm early, me early, and the morning kids, the ones always in their seats when I bust through the door out of breath and dragging ass and mayhem behind, their eyes watching, judging as I bump into desks on my way toward the back, are at the cafeteria, ordering hash browns from the short-order cooks, getting iced coffees, and looking at class notes. I want to cry.

This day is like a day that reminds me that I am missing. A face on a box of milk. That I am quiet, that I like Christmas dioramas and the art of Victorian children's books, that I like cats and dogs and flower shops. The Huntington Library and Arboretum. The Lotus Blossom Festival, field trips, and colored pencils. That I love to see plays. That if you ask me to show you my work, I would love to show it to you. That I would love your time. That I was once this other person, that I used to be.

"Well you're here early," says Ms. Lavoi walking up behind me. I realize I'm standing in front of the door to King Hall, staring into space, mouth open. I shake my head and walk with her.

"You get here kind of on the dot, don't you?" I ask, she opens the door to English and flips the lights, dumping her attaché and purse on the desk. She takes off her scarf and blazer, hangs them on the chair.

"I don't know." She shrugs. "I've got ten minutes, I was going to get a coffee, join me?"

"Sure."

"Have you had a chance to read the Plath?"

"Was that the book you recommended?"

"Oh, come on now," she says, sounding sassy, taking me to task. But all my nerves and emotions just want her to be nice, to be boring and a teacher. I want her to be something different, I don't want her to be like me.

"No. Not yet."

"Oh, well, when you do," she says, sensing my hurt. "Are you okay?" she asks, stopping. I stop too.

"Yeah, I just want to walk with you, if that's okay."

"Of course." And she starts up again. "What's your favorite book?"

"Mine?"

"Yes."

"Probably *Wuthering Heights*."

"Is that so? Did you read it here?"

"Yeah, last year in Sorenson."

"Well, what did you like about it?"

"The haunted vernacular." And she stops again.

"What are your plans after you leave here?"

"To be on Broadway."

"I'm being serious."

"So am I."

"Did you go to the Juilliard conference in the lecture hall?"

"No."

"How do you expect to get to New York?"

"I'm a junior, I still have next year."

"You have three months next year, then applications are due. This is something you should have started last semester."

Suddenly I don't want her to be a teacher anymore.

"Well I didn't. I haven't."

"What can I do to help you?" she asks, sounding so sincere it makes me uncomfortable.

"You can buy me coffee."

"I can manage that. Are you hungry? Do you need money for food?"

"No, it's not like that, I have stuff to eat. In my house, my mom, we're okay, mostly. Here, see." I pull out a bag of orange slices that I carefully cut and cleaned earlier. Brushing the seeds and juice into the trash, washing the cutting board and putting it back. Placing each one, piece by piece into the plastic bag, and twisting its top into a pigtail before dropping them into my purse.

I want to lie down in a large bed and be covered. I want someone to brush my hair behind my ear and temple with their fingers. I want someone to make me dinner, to be home when I get home, to live with me, around me, near me, to see me. I want to go back in time DeLorean-style, to a past I can't remember but feel withering away inside my bones.

×

"Ms. Darling! You join us," says Ms. Deaver, slapping her hand against today's script. She walks across the length of the stage to where I'm tossing my clothes and books into the front-row seats.

"Yes."

"Do you feel like singing?"

"I guess. Really?"

"Good, you're singing. Get onstage."

"Okay, sure," I say, smiling. Last semester was the last time I was asked to sing and never to start with the lead.

"You warmed up?"

"No."

"Warm up. Who else feels like getting up here? I've got both guys and gals in my hands people, come on let me hear some noise, everybody's welcome, grab a song," she holds out the music sheets, "don't be shy!"

In the back of the theater I see Joey Kandarian walk by, he sees me and waves. I turn around and lean forward, start to stretch, do my cherry pickers, I look between my legs and he's gone. I sigh and get back up.

"Don't stop! Keep picking!" shouts the Deaver. "It's just you today, Darling, you're singing the big one."

"What?" I ask, looking around.

"No takers. Just your little string-bean torso and big ole alto, I can even sort of remember what it sounds like, can't you?" she asks our ensemble filing in, bored, and dropping bags into the front row. No one answers because mostly know one cares and let's be honest, I'm a stranger here, a ghost. "Let's break. Nikki, run around the building and get ready. Everyone else, water, stretch, wait for a tap on the shoulder, I'm picking a guy at random. We're singing *Jesus Christ Superstar* today. We need a Carl Anderson, who will be our Carl Anderson today? Go!" She looks at me. "You're wearing sneakers, go!"

I jump off stage and push the black emergency-exit door into the bright outdoors. Kids from vocal are under the stage beams smoking and chatting. I lift up my feet and move. It feels good, my body in motion. I try to think about the last time I did something nice for it, other than give it water and occasional sleep.

I run past the dance hall, see the ballerinas and modern dancers, leaping and stretching, rising like slim, lithe cat toys, the kind tied to a string that snap back into place. Elegant ribbons cutting through the air. I take in a great swell of lung breath and feel it expand my chest, my ribs opening and closing, tiny rib-bone fingers playing here's-the-church, here's-the-steeple, giving and pulling inside, pulling and stretching. When I was a child, my mother was a runner. She'd wake up every morning before the sun and leave to sprint around the Rose Bowl, three miles all the way around, and watch the sun rise on the drive back home. I'd wait to hear the door open and shut, sigh, and fall asleep again, safe, knowing she had returned. When I was ten she invited me to join her and it was the thing I most enjoyed. The way the other runners ran alongside us, and the crunching of the oak leaves beneath our feet. The way the only thing you could hear was the sound of your own breath, pressing up through your chest, and in that winter, the first and last we ran, you could even see it puff before you, just a split second, before you left it behind. I turn toward the field, where the college students run and jump on the track, the pounding of my feet keeping time. I run between them, the grass on the lawn is wet and as my feet come down small bits of damp earth and dust stick to the moist sides of my shoes. I shake my neck from side to side and hop off the field around the bottom of the Republic of Smokey. I can see science students, not much older than myself, freshmen at most, filing in. I dart between them and start heading back toward the theater.

"Nicole Darling," calls a man's voice. I stop in place. "Ms. Darling." It's Mr. Gaines, the principal. I turn around, bring a hand to my forehead to block the sun, and stand, trying to catch my breath.

"Yeah?" I ask, leaning on one foot, the other hand on my burning side. The fire in my gut an aphrodisiac driving me to go further, do more. I can feel the pressure in my chest, the width of its expansion.

"Come with me," he says humorlessly, pulling his coat, which rests over his arm, tighter into his grasp.

"I'm on my way back to class," I wheeze.

"It can wait."

"Actually Ms. Deaver's expecting me. I'm supposed to sing."

"It can wait," he repeats, pointing toward his office on the bottom floor of the library.

"Okay," I say, dropping my arms and following him. He pulls open the office door and motions for me to enter.

"Is this going to take long?" I ask.

"Don't worry about that," he says. "Sit." He drops his briefcase and coat and gestures at the chair on the other side of his desk. He turns the blinds to keep the sun from glaring into the room. "I was on my way home," he says. "I'm glad I caught you." I look back toward the office behind me into the school courtyard and all of everything outside that's waiting. "I've been trying to get ahold of your mother," he says, opening the file cabinet behind his desk and pulling out a manila folder.

"Oh yeah?"

"Yes."

"Okay," I say, not sure what to say.

"You're aware that you were placed on attendance probation this semester?"

I shift in my seat, my chest slowly starting to decompress. My lungs growing steady and calm. I cough into my fist.

He opens the folder and pulls out a paper with my signature on it, *Nicole Rodríguez Darling*. It's my letter of acceptance, the one I signed two years ago. "This here," he says, pushing it across the table at me, "is a contract of agreement. An agreement that you take seriously the gift, really the investment the city of Los Angeles is making in you. A free top-tier college preparatory education, plus the best arts program in the state." I look down at the paper, March 1994, the year I got the letter in the mail. The day I threw myself into my mother's arms sobbing. "I'm going to make it," I cried, "I'm really going to do it." I slept in her bed that night and kissed my cat. I could hardly sleep. So much seemed to await, I felt unafraid. All that summer I jogged and sang, studied monologues I bought from Cliff's Books, taking the bus to find new playwrights. Come August I was ready, the first in line, standing in the front of class.

"Do you know how many unexcused absences you've had this semester?"

"No," I answer, pushing the letter back.

"Are you aware that there is a waiting list to get into this school? That you are being funded by an endowment?"

"Yes."

He sighs and tucks the letter back into my file. Folds his hands on the desk and looks at me, he looks sad, like this is harder for him. Like this is really painful stuff. I feel a tear slide loose and wipe it away quickly. He grabs a box of Kleenex by the pens and hands it over. I take it carefully. "I'm afraid," he starts, fear seizes my chest and I bury my face in my hands and shake my head.

"No," I choke.

"I'm so sorry. Have your mother call me, please," he says softly, and then stands. "By the end of this week." I stand too. "You're free to go. Tell Ms. Deaver I apologize for your delay."

Inside the theater I walk quickly to the front row and grab my things. Ms. Deaver's face changes when she sees mine. "Nicole," she calls. I walk-jog toward the exit door. I don't stop and sure as hell don't look back.

×

Gas Food Lodging, Allison Anders, gorgeous love letter to a small New Mexican town and teenage weirdness, her stamp of approval on feelings that like swamps grab you by the ankles and pull you deeper into the muck of sadness, is showing at the Rialto and I'm wiping away tears to see it. The theater is empty and I watch Shade, the film's heroine, watch. We watch together. Someone told me the movie was based on a book so I went a while back to the main Pasadena library branch, the really big beautiful one on Walnut, with the quotes of the philosophers carved into the stone walls. I checked it out. *Don't Look and It Won't Hurt* is what the book is called. Written by a guy named Richard Peck. I flipped it over in my hand, looking for his picture, but it wasn't there. So I had nothing to go on but his words. And what words they were. It made me trust men a little more. A tiny spoonful. I know that not all men have to be strangers, not all men are blind. It's nothing like the movie though with Shade and her sweaters, her David Bowie posters and loss. Rocks that glow beneath the light. And their life never seems that empty, never seems that sad, but it seems familiar and so I guess it must be, I guess it is. I remember when it came out, seeing the commercials on TV. I was younger then, of course. We have caught up with one another, Shade and I, sixteen and all these feelings in a lump. The glowing red eyes of the sphinxes affixed to the corners of the Rialto like the Southern Oracle in *The Neverending Story*, light the edges of the screen, the old art deco design, the balcony that is never used anymore, but was built for a piano, when films were silent and the noises that happened, the sound of thunder and suspense were a symphony of keys, pressing down from the heavens, the wooden eaves.

I grab my pager and it's too late. I've missed all of Arts. It's inevitable, this long drawn-out process. This is what the moms cry about on *Ricki Lake*, what they want to pull their thirteen-year-old snotty daughters from the brink of. This thing that sort of feels like this. It's *hollowed out*. Like if I swallowed someone they'd just keep falling and I'd never hear a plop.

I look behind me toward the projector booth. There's no sexy misunderstood cholo running the reel, not like in the movie, who really turns out to be a fifth-generation Nuevo Mexicano, just like me, and not a cholo at all, with a deaf mom who dances to the vibrations coming up from the floor.

I half expect it to be raining and gray when I push into the outdoors, but it's not, it's sunny. It's four thirty and all the birds are still doing their bird thing. I've taken a risk, coming to South Pasadena on a school day in the afternoon because they're real fascists about ditching and the town's just small enough for the cops to get bored and give a shit. But most schools get out at three and by now I'm safe.

I walk down the street in no particular direction, the leaves ripple and fan themselves, spring tosses up its pollens. In the eighties all sorts of teen movies were filmed here because it's one of the only places in the city without palm trees obscuring every view and the bungalows are turn of the century and East Coast looking. *Teen Wolf*, *Pretty in Pink*, *Teen Witch*. Just two years ago Dan's neighbor's house was used as Angela Chase's for *My So-Called Life*. Sarah and I saw Jared Leto and Claire Danes walking the streets like tourists on the moon, pausing in front of the library like they were in Mayberry and not Los Angeles. Tilting their heads at the red bricks and smoke from chimneys, rubbing their sneakered feet into the yellow and orange leaves cluttering up the sidewalks.

I weave slowly, arms out like I'm flying, toward the McDonald's and pause. The last time I ate here was in eighth grade, before Ry told me about vivisection and pig snouts and grody cow eyeballs plucked out with the torturous tongs of capitalism. Last Halloween, Sarah and I were driving around smoking weed like dummies, when we saw Jessica, Chelo, and Dan swinging and hanging off the McDonald's mini merry-go-round, they jumped off, laughing and stumbling up the sidewalk.

"Hey, pull over," I said to her. "It's Dan." "No," she answered, "he's with Consuelo and Jess Silverman." "So," I said, turning the wheel toward the curb, double baked and potato stuffed. "Stop it!" she shrieked, pulling my hand off. "What's wrong with them?" I asked, watching as they turned the corner toward the residential part of town and disappeared into a sea of tiny ghosts and pirates. "They're weird," she answered. "Weird how?" "I don't know, they just are." And we kept driving. Later Dan told me they were tripping balls and trying to find Garfield Park and by the time they made it the sun was coming up. They huddled inside the concrete tube in the playground and touched each other's faces until they fell asleep. "You weren't hassled by a single pig?" I asked. "Nope," he answered, packing a bowl. "Not a single one."

×

I'm at Los Tacos on Fair Oaks eating nachos when I see Sarah jump off the bus across the street. I heard Marc's car busted a radiator and she's been back on public transport.

I know she's going to the West Coast Video instead of the Blockbuster by home because she loves the cult section and will often take the transfer just to get something good. From its trove of the radical we've seen *The Decline of Western Civilization, American Pop*, all the Bakshi classics, *Heathers, Das Boot, The Damned, Night of the Living Dead, Parents*, new episodes of *Tales from the Crypt. Casablanca, The Holy Mountain, The Conversation*, and every Argento and Varda we could get our hands on.

I lick my fingers, toss my tray, and jog across the street, pull open the big glass door and head for our aisle. She's wearing green faded bell-bottoms, Jack Purcells, and a tight vintage baseball shirt. Her dark hair is loose and flaps all over the place. Growing up people thought we were sisters. One time at The Hat, while sharing chili fries, as her father sat a few tables away reading the *Star News*, an older man in a plaid shirt buttoned at the cuffs and gray work slacks slid into our booth and said that we looked like Romanian princesses from a fairy tale. What the actual fuck. We were eleven. Sarah very elegantly tilted her head and pushed her hair behind one ear and bit her lower lip. Both embarrassed and invisible, and the brightest thing in the room, I wished my body could evaporate into a cloud. A place where I could wave a hand over my face and make it disappear.

The next year she fucked Marc's grody bandmate. He pulled her jeans down to her ankles in their basement, did it standing up while holding her neck, on the stairs, against the *Animals* album poster. Or at least that's what she says.

"Howdy!" I say too cartoonish and she looks down hurt. "Hey," I counter, softer. She sets *Cannibal Corpse* back and walks to the other side of the aisle, so we are facing one another like Pyramus and Thisbe, like Romeo and Juliet, divided and un-united.

She doesn't say anything and continues to read the back of another box. *Rocky Horror*. "Hey," I say again, running my finger along the top of the divider. "Can we talk? You've seen that."

"Why?" She puts Janet and Dr. Frank-N-Furter back, finally looking up. She crosses her arms and seems bored. Not mean or anything, just bored, and I fucking hate her.

"Because I was an asshole."

"Tell me something I don't know."

"I'm just making new friends is all."

"Yeah, I get it and don't give a shit. Just, when we're together don't treat me like an idiot who doesn't know anything. And don't act like I'm always bothering you. You're the one that comes to my house all the time complaining about stuff."

"That's fair."

"Ugh, why do you talk like that? Like a fucking therapist."

"I'm a philosopher."

"Shut up, this isn't a joke, don't treat me like an asshole."

"Fine, what do you want?"

"For you to grow a pair of fucking tits and say you're sorry."

"I think I've got the tit part covered." She rolls her eyes and keeps walking down the aisle. "I get it."

"Later dude," she says heading toward the door.

"Wait," I say walking behind her. We're outside now on the asphalt. She covers her eyes as if blocking the sun but I don't know why if she isn't standing in its blindness. She tries to speak but it comes out all gobbledy-gunk. I realize she's crying.

"Are you crying?"

"You are so hard to understand!" she says, bringing her arm down in a sad gesture of frustration. It hits me that she's really pissed. Really, really pissed. And it stuns me into silence.

"I'm not sure what to say." I am constantly surprised that anything I say or do can make anyone feel anything.

"Say you're sorry."

"Sarah, I didn't do anything wrong." She turns around and hurries up to the corner and I walk after her. The light turns green and we walk side by side toward Memorial Park, her trying to outpace me. The Aztec mural, yellow and vibrant blue, flashes me back to childhood. Looking for Easter eggs. "Tell me what I did! I don't understand."

She stops. "Dude, you are so bent mentally. I swear. You really let school do a fucking number on you. I don't know, you get high all the time."

"So do you! Hypocrite! So do you!"

"I don't do what other stuff you're doing, tweak, huffing, what the fuck, man. You're like a Hollywood cling-on, you hang out with all those weird industry kids and those,

those, punks who I just, I don't know you anymore, I guess."

"I'm finding my tribe, you know?"

"You're rude, you never return my phone calls, you insult me to my face, you make fun of everything I do. I mean, what the fuck Nikki, you can't even see what a shithead you are? Honestly? How am I Heather and you're Big Fun? That makes no fucking sense!"

I laugh despite myself and she does too. I remember that she's funny, that there's a reason we're friends. I know I need to do this thing even if it's contrary to my heart. Even if what she's threatened by is my own dislocation in her life, even if I can't explain my anger, even if I can't unshake this gloom, even if I die thirty years later, liver pickled and sour, bags beneath my eyes, a raccoon princess stuffed with garbage, thin white maggots spilling from my lips, addiction tucking me in forever like the mother I never had.

"Okay. Okay. I'm sorry. Jesus."

She exhales and wipes under her eyes and takes a deep breath. "Okay, thank you. I can't hug, is that cool?"

"Whatever," I say. We walk into the park and sit. She's snotty and I look at my hands while she fixes herself.

"Are you cool?" she asks, finally looking up.

"Yeah, I'm cool."

"No, I mean, yeah, you are cool. It's weird. For me."

"Oh," I say, understanding what she means. "Sorry."

"Do you like it?"

"I don't know. I don't think so. I'm sad, mostly."

"I saw your dad's car. Is he in town?"

"He was. He left. He was visiting my uncle and stopped by to say hi."

"Oh." She twists a silver turquoise ring around her finger. "I saw Lyla."

"Yeah, she's there."

"How long?"

I shrug. "Dunno."

"Look," she says. "I think I should go."

"Okay," I say, looking up as she stands.

"I'm glad we talked."

"Okay."

And then she stands there a minute, looking at me, as if I'm supposed to say something, only I have no idea what.

"Have you ever thought you might be a sociopath?" she asks, and I laugh.

"What? Seriously?"

"Yes."

"I don't even think I know what that is."

"It's when you don't see your own shitty actions as being shitty and live in a sort of unawareness of how you might hurt or affect other people."

"See, I just don't understand that."

"Yeah, well. Exactly."

"You're really being serious."

"Okay," she says softly. "Bye, Nikki."

I feel something inside my chest jostle and a strong wave of it washes over my head and I'm high on it. A thin film of gray. "Bye, Sarah." And she fades away.

×

I pick up the phone and dial. I'm sitting on the washing machine in Grandpa's old room, which is Lyla's new room that she hasn't been staying in. Staying instead somewhere in the Valley with some friend of our cousin, and Mom is sick about it. I've been masturbating with the electric back massager and listening to death metal. Specifically Nausea, which Dan turned me on to. It rings a few times then he picks up. "Yo," he answers.

"Is your mom in Venice?"

"Till Monday."

"Do you want company?"

"Like, to blaze?"

"No, like, to make friendship bracelets."

"Yeah, come over, we can make lanyards."

"Okay, rad. I'll bring the trust fall. You get the canoe. Oh, hey, I have Thin Mints. Got 'em outside the Ralphs."

"Uh, his name is Raaaaaallpphh," Dan says Cheech-style and we both laugh.

×

"Daniel Martínez, did you take a shower?"

"Oh yeah," he says, touching the tips of his wet hair, "don't tell anyone," and flashes an award-winning smile.

"Anyway," I say packing a new bowl. The night is groovy and we talk amongst his posters and books. The Ramones' *Rocket to Russia,* Garbage Pail Kids thumbtacked to the wall, Big Gulps like small moat towers guard the bed.

"Nausea is not that metal sounding."

"That's because it's not metal. You're packing it wrong, you gotta press it in more otherwise it blows out."

"Blows out or blows out?"

"Like, away," he says, grabbing the pipe from me and jamming the weed into the bowl with dirty fingers. "It's hardcore. I told you that."

"Oh. Well I don't like it."

"I knew you wouldn't."

"What does that mean?"

He sparks up. "You talk too much, Nik." He smiles slowly, weirdly. "Hey, you want a beer?"

I do but I don't. "Maybe," I say. My heart races and I grab for the weed. My pulse is a thing. He stands and walks to the hall, comes back, and sits next to me on the bed. He cracks one and I get goose bumps as he places it in my hand, beads of water sprouting on my palm.

"It means you only like the Pixies and shit like that."

"That's not true, I like punk. Real punk, like the Misfits and the Cramps."

"You like all that twangy rockabilly 'Rat Fink' shit. That's all musical theater, of course you like that shit. You don't like destruction."

"Oh don't I?" I ask, taking a gulp. Beer is so gross. "I love destruction. I think it's fucked and brilliant. I think it's way more complex than anyone talks about."

"I do too. I think it's bunk and refreshing."

I laugh. "Way bunk."

"The Bunky Bunch." He blows smoke and takes my chin. His fingers are warm and we've paused.

"I'm a virgin," I whisper. I don't even want this, I just want something different than what I've got.

"I know," he says, pressing his mouth to mine, passing the smoke. He exhales and I pull away. Hold it in. "We talk about it all the time. Blow." I do and he sparks the pipe, takes a new hit, inhales. He gestures for me and I lean in, he blows I hold. "Blow." I do and he places his hands on my neck lightly, his thumbs pressing into the crest of my breasts. "We should fix that," he whispers. I soften and everything around me speeds up again and his tongue is moving in and out of my mouth and we lie back, him on top and he's taking off his pants, shoving his legs out of them and then mine and he's hard. I gasp. I feel him on my stomach and it's strange and unreal. My friend Dan has his naked dick on my stomach. I've never been pressed up against life like this. I see him in the motel, the bathroom door swinging open, his friend, blond girl, sad and weepy on the toilet seat, he starts to knead his hips against mine, his hand pushing my legs apart gently yet persistently, moving his other hand toward my shirt, trying to pull it over my head, he's in motion tethered to nothing and suddenly I understand, he's good at this, he excels. I see him on the couch at parties, girls melting into his side. He's Peter Pan with a needle and thread and I'm his shadow. He starts to move faster, more aggressively, his hand is in my bra sort of massaging my nipple, his eyes are open and we catch each other and he doesn't smile, we don't make a weird face or laugh, he seems outside himself, otherworldly and I want to tell him, *I can just hug you instead*, but I don't.

"You're gorgeous," some strange voice I don't recognize says and I turn my face to deflect the compliment because it seems ill-suited to my current nakedness. He's on his knees, completely hard, veins and arms and feet and phallus. He is a statue, the Rodins outside the Norton Simon. His sandpaper fingers slip inside, I gasp, ripples rising on my body, tiny alarm sensors going off. I see his Garbage Pail poster, Diaper Dan, on the ceiling above us. *Diaper Dan*. I shove him off and he topples onto the floor with an unsexy thump, like in a romantic comedy I'd be forced to watch on an airplane. I freeze, motionless. *Disbelief* would best describe his look. I cover my face. I hate every second of this. "What is wrong with you!" he finally shouts and I roll over, stunted by his anger. I don't say anything just lie there, staring at him. He stands, dick soft, and pulls his underwear on. He walks into the bathroom and slams the door. "Fucking go home!" he shouts.

"I'm sorry," I say, gathering my clothes. "I'm so sorry. I got scared."

"Go home, Nicole," he says from behind the door, this time louder, more insistent.

"Are you mad at me?"

"Can you go the fuck home?" he shouts again and this time it shakes me into motion. I pull my clothes on and walk through the house toward the front door and survey the surroundings as if on a movie set. The fridge is buzzing and I open it. Inside a twenty-four pack of Bud Light, a block of cheddar cheese, some tortillas, and Oreos. The counter space is covered in SpaghettiOs cans, ashtrays, and fallen soldiers. I take a gulp of air and look behind me toward the back of the small Spanish bungalow, where Dan has lived unattended for nearly three years. His mother's boyfriend's house. One of two, the one he lives in while they stay together at the other house in Venice and his older brother and father survive in El Monte working odd jobs trying to get by. Dan has gone to good schools. Maybe this Spanish Bungalow was the one that got him into the right school district. Before he transferred to LACHSA. Maybe this was his mother's bottom line. Her only demand. There is so much that I don't know about anything or anyone. Like, how did your life get this way? When did it pivot to the place it is now? Was it hard to say goodbye? Did you know that goodbye was even coming? I want to go back and sit with him, hold his hand and say, *It's all right. I'm alone too.* Watch *Bill and Ted*, get baked, and sleep beside one another. But I don't. I open the front door and walk into the windy street toward the car, the streetlights fluttering, the edge of South Pasadena, the last city before Los Angeles, the border of the SGV, the Santa Anas kicking up the dusty screams of all of us, gathering them together like a party, just to blow them out into our faces.

I drive home in a daze and swear to god as I turn the corner onto my street, signs blowing hectic against the storm, a coyote emerges from the dust, eyes shining, and gallops toward the hills.

×

A glare of sunlight fills the length of King Hall. Everything is empty and it's early, well, not so early. Class is in session. I'm not sure if I've been kicked out. My mom hasn't called Principal Gaines and I haven't spoken to her. They'll have to track her down and until then I'm still coming. You'll have to drag me out of here, motherfuckers. My backpack is over my shoulder and I walk carefully past the classroom windows, not to let the teachers see me. The faces of my comrades looking up with rapt attention. School. Heh. What a joke. Or maybe not. I long painfully to want nothing more than just good grades. It seems so long since I've felt an order to the universe. In fact, I'm convinced I've never felt it. Cruelty is the randomness with which life picks its victims. I am the least of its struggling and yet I feel its weight. All around me, on my shoulders, caught inside my throat, pressing on the backside of my neck. What am I doing trying to stay in this place. They're doing me a favor. I should hop the fence, toss my books behind me, and run wild into the sunset. Hitchhike to New York and never look back. When you're from LA, where else do you go?

The sun makes everything silhouettes, but even in the brightness that surrounds her Claire's body is clear to me. The long thin arms toned. I know that she is from Alhambra. I know that she is a broken mold, her former husk lying on some nighttime road, with skateboards and broken 40s, cluttering up the gutters with its fragile shape. I know that she has been playing clarinet for many years.

That her mother came here to have her sister who was inside her, and who was challenging the one-child rule, and whose secret sonogram confirmed her gendered doom. I know Claire worked at Claire's at the Montebello Town Center and everyone thought this was really funny and that she was fired for stealing an ear-piercing gun. I know that Claire is beautiful and that people say she's mean. I know she doesn't like many people. I know that Claire might like me and I've clung to this, I've clung to it as evidence that might incriminate me, but only to myself.

At the end of the hall in front of her locker she looks like a movie poster for some sad flick about high school kids at risk, like *Lean on Me*, or *Stand and Deliver*. Like Claire's got some lesson to teach us all, except the lessons Claire would teach aren't the lessons being taught by the people in charge. And that's why Claire isn't a movie poster. That's why Claire is real. That's why I am real. That's why all of this is so much more than shapes and shadows. I close my eyes, open them, and Claire is gone. The lockers are now metal chairs with thick vinyl green plastic I can feel, sweaty beneath thin bare child legs poking through my shorts. I'm in the hallway of the hospital. The morning sun rises through a grated window high along the wall. A prison I will never leave. My parents' voices which at one point were both so clear are now and forever garbled beneath the water of our future lives and nothing they will ever say makes sense again.

When I was five years old my sister killed herself. Lori. She was Lyla's twin. She was twelve. She'd had a fight with dad and things must have been bad for her.

I say *must have* because we have never once as a family talked about it, her, even individually to one another. We talk around it, we say things aimed at it but never close enough to hit the mark. In this way we have never stopped talking about it. I wonder if my thinking about it and writing about it and imagining it is my way of trying to be sure it ever happened. If she existed at all or was just a memory I manifested. The picture basket has never had a single photo of her and I know my mother has gone through and removed them all. The only face of hers I see are baby pictures with Lyla where they are shoved together like otters, floating on their backs. She is a paranormal presence like the TV in *Poltergeist* and I hold my hands up to movies, books, and air trying to find her. Feel her. She slit her wrists after coming home from school one day. She was in the seventh grade. It was quiet, sunlight turning on the ceiling across the floor. I was in the living room, on the avocado-colored carpet, watching *Mr. Rogers*, the large window bright with midafternoon sun, the river in the distance, the thick cluster of bright green tops pushing against dark clouds, black crows swirling against the wind. My mother's shriek fills every pore of our home, every tiny minutia of our home, our clothing, our toys, our food, our air, our pillows, our pockets, our memories, our mouths, are filled and will be filled always with that scream. We are drunk in it.

My father is on his feet flying into the house from the garage where he's been building a bike. He's followed us after the long drive to Los Angeles, after a summer of living with our grandparents in New Mexico, after three months of saving, we came back to LA, and after all of that he followed us, and she let him in. "It's his father's house," she shrugged, "after all." My mom is in my sister's doorway now, heaving and covering her mouth, my dad pushes past her and starts yelling and moaning, "No, oh no, no," loud embarrassing sounds I wish he wasn't making, she's in his arms, Lori, his face is contorted and white, her wrists exit first, flapping around her flag uniform, polyester and soaked bright violet red. It's drippy, my mom is spinning in on herself down the hall. My father hoists Lori over his shoulder like a heavy bag of cement and is on the phone. Her eyes are whites and she sees me, hanging upside down, she moves her mouth, she's hanging and upside down it looks like a smile. I shake my head and cover my eyes. My mother grabs me and I'm tossed on my bed, the door slams.

When my grandmother pulled me out of the corner of the room I was surprised to see my things, my dolls, my toys and bed, and know that they weren't really mine. The person they belonged to didn't know them anymore. They had transformed, like the Velveteen Rabbit. Turned real overnight and everything they had been before didn't matter after that.

I'm on a couch in front of a television, neighbor Margaret is asleep in her velvet-blue recliner, her mouth ajar, I am watching Sunday Night Disney, it's a rerun, Walt, the 1960s, his vision. He says, "Tomorrow," like it's a place we might get to. A set of plans, the old faces, the old names, animatronic magic, a diorama of a fantasy he wants to bring to life. The door opens and it's my mother. She raises her finger to my lips and scoops me up.

Lyla has been taken to a psychiatric ward. She walks out in a paper gown, like I've seen on *General Hospital*. She looks different. My mother gets up from where we've been waiting and walks to her. They hug. My sister looks at me and her face, right side up, is frowning. My dad is in the hallway on the pay phone talking to my grandmother. He sees Lyla and sets the phone on top of the counter with the phone book. He walks to me and sits. Takes my hand and pats it softly, staring forward. My sister sees us and starts down the long hallway with my mother who has placed an arm around her shoulder and guides her slowly. My father stands, pauses, then follows.

"Your grandmother is on her way," he says and then he too is engulfed in the shadow of the hallway. I sit and look at the flat Easter baskets taped to the wall. Fuzzy to the touch, pastel-colored eggs inside. The kind inside my kindergarten classroom. Other girls walk through, they are in gray sweats and pop gum, shuffle by in slippers, they have Bibles and *Bop* magazines and banana clips and friendship bracelets in neon pink and green. The fluorescent lights buzz and blink, the linoleum blue gold and gray, flecked and shining.

My grandmother Gail is beside me. "Don't ever need to come here," she whispers, lifting me into her arms, and we're headed toward the parking lot, the gray sky still swirling, wetness hanging from all the tree things.

Blackbirds peck at rainbow puddles of oil and water, and the sun, a spool of gold glowing in the sky, blinds me with confusion. And I never do.

When I was very small Lori snuck into my room, opened the window, jumped out, turned around, held a finger to her lips and said, "Shhh." I had no idea she meant forever.

"Hey," I say, leaning down beside Claire.

"Hey," she says, without looking up. She's got an honest-to-god motherfucking hospital bracelet on and I gulp.

"You wear that thing to look cool?"

She glares at me and rolls her eyes, holding a History book. "Nikki," and I jump, hearing my name in her mouth. "I know your name, asshole." I nod. "You got very bitter very quickly," is all she follows it up with and turns back to the locker rummaging around and pulling out old papers and assignments, a small Beanie Baby cat with the Ty tag still on. She rips off a magnet mirror, a fake California license plate with her name on it, CLAIRE. A palm tree sticker beside a pink cup that holds glitter bubble ink pens. She shoves these things into her backpack.

"What does that mean?" I ask softly, unsure.

"Never mind," she says flipping her hair.

"No, I mean . . ."

"What do you want from me? What are you standing here gawking at me for? You want some wise ching-chong wisdom?"

"God Claire, come on. I'm not like that."

"Sure, sure. No one is. I'm the one who's crazy. I'm the bitch."

"Are you okay? I mean, no one's seen you all semester, how you left it was, really intense. I just want to know that you're okay."

"Why?"

"God, I don't know. Because I care about you. I miss you. I mean, I miss you being at school."

She blows her bangs out of her face and stares at me. "You want to know that things are going to be okay? *The future's so bright you gotta wear shades?* Look I don't know. My mom is downstairs and I'm going back. Don't get wiggy in the hallways, that's all I'm saying."

"That's what Chelo said."

"Consuelo Medina?"

"Yeah."

"What a biter. I said that shit first."

I don't know what she means by this, that Chelo could somehow be a lesser person, a person someone like Claire thinks is uncool, that anyone could think Chelo is desperate, desperate enough to bite anyone else to make herself sound cooler, but also because now I'm not sure if it was déjà vu, or if in fact Chelo ever said this, and that frightens me. Claire tilts her head and a softness tugs at the edges of her mouth and she kind of more or less seems to understand that something bigger is going on and in this moment decides to be straight with me, and that in this straightness she is being kind.

"It's not going to be okay if that's what you're sort of poorly asking. I'm sorry. It's shit, all of it. And they want you to feel stupid."

"Okay," I say nodding, understanding this. "They do?"

"They do, all of them, they don't care. You should have seen the way they took me out of here."

"I did."

"Yeah, well."

"I'm sorry they did that to you."

"Look, if you're anything like me, this place is a real drag. Don't, you know, kill yourself over it or whatever. Or, kill yourself."

"I don't want to kill myself."

"Good."

"Do you, want to . . ."

"Look, I gotta go, my mom's downstairs. I just mean, don't wait for anything to get better. Nothing gets better for us. You know? I guess just do what they say and be who you are later."

"When is later?"

"I don't know. Later I guess, when we're grown-ups, when we're on our own."

"Okay. Good luck."

"Thanks. I gotta go." And she slams the locker shut and stands. "It's really shitty, I know."

"Can I ask you something else?"

"Sure, but make it snappy." She brushes long swaths of black hair away from her face, her Adidas body-hugging jersey pulling up from her shorty-short raver shorts.

"Were you ever happy, even when you were a kid?"

"Sure, a few times. Not enough I guess." At this she sort of snort-laughs as if remembering something only she can see, and it's weird because I've never seen her laugh before and her smile is glorious.

"So is it scary there? At the hospital?" And now she's the one that looks confused.

"I'm not in a hospital. I'm in rehab." She holds out the plastic bracelet as evidence and something like panic and hopelessness swarms up from the pit of my gut, my chest constricts, nothing I know is true and I am so unsure. About everything. Memories, people, events, a blur of pops and flashes. "I'm not crazy, Nikki, and neither are you. Who the fuck else were we supposed to become in a world full of all of them?" She turns and walks calmly back down the hall, head drooped, hair a shroud around her shoulders, into the light that opens like a window and she's taken all the air with her, now that she has gone.

With gratitude:

There are so many people to thank for this book, I'm overwhelmed to think where to begin.

First and foremost, Laurie Pike. Thank you, Laurie, for taking a chance on a crazy teenage kid, believing in me, pushing me to succeed, introducing me to cultural icons and just subculture in general, and showing me a vision of a life I wanted. Thank you for saying, this is for you, this can be yours.

Jessica Hopper, Ann Powers, Chris Ziegler, Randall Roberts.

Every English teacher I've ever had. Pasadena City College, Eugene Lang College. Maggie Nelson, Janet Sarbanes, and the entire CalArts writing faculty.

USC and my cohort. My committee, Dana Johnson, Aimee Bender, Karen Tongson, Laura Isabel Serna, Tania Modleski.

Raquel Gutiérrez, Kate Wolf, Daniel Ingroff, Paul Pescador, David Gilbert, Samantha Cohen, Charlotte Harrigan, Ann Friedman, Stacy Wood, Sarah Williams, Carolyn Pennypacker Riggs, Jessie Thurston, Jibade-Khalil Huffman, Dean Erdmann, Mark McKnight, Whitney Hubbs,

Beth Pickens, Asher Hartman, Amanda Yates Garcia, Jaye Fishel, John Burtle, Emi Fontana, Paul Soto, Rachel Kaadzi Ghansah.

Megan McGinnis and Michelle Pullman.

Marissa López and the UCLA Chicano Studies Research Center.

Michelle Tea and the Feminist Press, RADAR Productions, Juliana Delgado Lopera, Virgie Tovar, and the 2016 Sister Spit crew.

My family, Nancy Darling and Bud Darling who are not the parents in this novel and have always supported and believed in me. My sister Anna Marie, Ananda Day Cavalli and her family, my tía Lily Martínez and all my ancestors in New Mexico. My grandparents Maria and Rufus Rodríguez. The Darling family, my cousins Itzel and Nayeli Lavanderos, my tía Cindy Hawes.

Mari, Angie, Adam, Belinda, and Sarah, wherever life takes us on this lumpy bumpy psychedelic trip, I carry you always and forever in my heart.

More Contemporary Fiction
from the Feminist Press

La Bastarda by Trifonia Melibea Obono,
translated by Lawrence Schimel

Black Wave by Michelle Tea

Give It to Me by Ana Castillo

Go Home! edited by Rowan Hisayo Buchanan

Into the Go-Slow by Bridgett M. Davis

Love War Stories by Ivelisse Rodriguez

Maggie Terry by Sarah Schulman

Pretty Things by Virginie Despentes,
translated by Emma Ramadan

Since I Laid My Burden Down by Brontez Purnell

Though I Get Home by YZ Chin

Training School for Negro Girls by Camille Acker

We Were Witches by Ariel Gore

The Feminist Press is a nonprofit educational organization founded to amplify feminist voices. FP publishes classic and new writing from around the world, creates cutting-edge programs, and elevates silenced and marginalized voices in order to support personal transformation and social justice for all people.

See our complete list of books at
feministpress.org